Best Wishes
Maggie Gibson

GRACE, the HOOKER, the HARD-MAN and the KID

GRACE, the HOOKER, the HARD-MAN and the KID

MAGGIE GIBSON

POOLBEG

Published in 1995 by
Poolbeg Press Ltd,
Knocksedan House,
123 Baldoyle Industrial Estate,
Dublin 13, Ireland

A catalogue record for this book is available from the British Library.

ISBN 1 85371 433 X

Cover photography by Mike O'Toole
Cover design by Poolbeg Group Services Ltd
Set by Poolbeg Group Services Ltd in New Baskerville 10.5/13
Printed by The Guernsey Press Ltd,
Vale, Guernsey, Channel Islands.

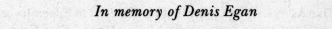

In memory of Denis Egan

Acknowledgements

Thanks to Katy Egan, my first reader. And to Eileen Joyce and Paul Davie for technical help. Also to Kate Cruise O'Brien for having faith!

About the Author

Maggie Gibson was born in Yorkshire of Irish parents. She now owns her own hairdressing business in Westport, Co Mayo. Her salon and home are in the house that her great-great-great-great-grandfather built in 1805.

Chapter One

The persistent ringing of the bedside phone dragged Grace by the roots of her hair from sleep. She reached out for it, anxious to stop the brain-jarring noise but instead succeeded in swiping it onto the floor. She cursed and leaned over the side of the bed to grab the receiver.

"Yes . . . What?"

"Grace?"

"What d'you want Doyle, I'm not on till two," she snapped, recognising the voice of Garda Sean Doyle at the other end of the line.

The ensuing stifled snigger didn't improve her disposition. "Hatchett wants you to go and interview a woman on the Ballycoyle estate. She's reported her daughter missing and . . . "

"Why me? . . . I've only been off duty five hours . . . Sod off, Doyle and get someone else."

"Right you are, Grace, I'll pass on your message to Inspector Hatchett."

"OK, OK . . . " she said quickly before he could ring off. "What's the address?"

The Ballycoyle estate sits uneasily on the south-west side of Dublin, the high-rise blocks and low-rise low-cost houses a constant monument to the worst planning mistakes of the sixties. The cracked concrete roads meander off at unlikely tangents round open once grassy areas where the kids play in burnt-out cars, and scrawny dogs sniff and snap at each other.

Grace cruised down Mimosa Park, along Cherry Orchard Avenue, and as usual got lost. She cursed to herself and reversed the car, heading back in the opposite direction. Eventually she stopped, and winding down the window called to a young woman in tight jeans and woolly coat who was tottering along on high white sling-backed sandals pushing a buggy containing a screaming child. The woman directed her back along Mimosa Park and miraculously two streets later she pulled up in front of three Nirvana Grove.

The front garden of Ann Power's council house was like an oasis in a desert of decay. The lush green of the tiny lawn was striped like a bowling green and colourful spring flowers spilled over onto the narrow flagstone path which led in two strides to the blue front door.

Four or five scruffy kids were leaping on and off the carcass of a burnt-out car, the wheels were missing and three of the hubs were propped up on concrete slabs. The biggest of the boys, who looked all of six or seven, scrambled onto the boot and across the roof whooping and yelling. The others followed the leader as he jumped onto the bonnet making the unsupported wheel hub rock violently in mid-air bouncing them all to the ground roaring and laughing.

She felt a tug at her sleeve and looked down at a pint-sized entrepreneur with a terminally runny nose.

"Look after yer car, missus?" The others ran over to join him, looking for a piece of the action.

"How much?" she asked.

"A fiver."

Grace snorted. "Get lost . . . a pound."

The boy looked round at his friends who were lounging against the wall watching him. "Two pound fifty," he said leaving a snail trail on his sleeve as he wiped it across his nose.

"One fifty."

"Two quid."

"Done," said Grace. "A pound now and another when I come back." The boy spat on the palm of his filthy hand and slapped it on Grace's after she had handed over the coin. The negotiator and his gang headed back to finish the game and Grace wiped her hand on her jeans as she walked up Ann Power's path.

Ann answered on the second ring, her eyes red from crying, her cheeks tear-stained. She invited Grace into her front sitting-room.

"The guards were here already today. I told them . . . I gave them a photograph . . . " She was a slight nervous woman, lighting the next cigarette from the last, talking in short staccato bursts.

"Yes I know, Mrs Power, I'm here . . . "

"Miss," interrupted Ann Power.

"Sorry?"

"It's Miss Power . . . Ann. I'm not married."

Grace nodded. "Fine . . . Ann . . . I'm here to talk to you about your daughter, to see if we can find out about her friends or her usual haunts, that kind of thing."

"She has no friends," said Ann bursting into tears. Grace managed to calm her after a while by making her a cup of tea. And they sat together on the country cottage settee while she gave details of the last time she had seen her only daughter when she had sent her to the supermarket the previous evening to do the weekly shopping.

"Why didn't you report her missing last night, Ann? Why did you wait until this morning?"

Ann Power wrapped her arms round her body and started to rock backwards and forwards where she sat. "I've no phone," she said with an air of helplessness.

"And I couldn't go out in the dark."

Ann was about forty and had definitely seen better days. Patches of psoriasis covered her bare legs and arms and from time to time she was convulsed with a smoker's cough. She had a quiet middle-class accent, which surprised Grace the first time she heard her speak. Her general appearance and the fact that she lived on the Ballycoyle estate predisposing her to expect a strong Dublin accent.

Ann lapsed into silence so Grace coaxed, "You have a very pretty home, do you do the garden yourself?"

Ann shook her head. "No, my father comes over to do it, I don't go out much." She folded her arms and hugged herself again. Grace nodded sympathetically and was about to speak when Ann went on in a rush. "I was waiting for her to come home to bring my cigarettes . . . she never came. She wouldn't leave me without cigarettes, not my Nicky . . . " she trailed off, looking pleadingly at Grace, willing her to give her some good news.

"Do you know if Nicky is friendly with any one at all?"

"Nicky kept to herself . . . she found life easier that way. The bullying you understand."

"She was bullied at school?"

Ann, picking at an imaginary piece of lint on her skirt, kept her eyes averted from Grace's. "It was her accent, she was different . . . you know what children can be like."

"Do you think she could have run away, Ann, do you think that maybe she just couldn't take it any more?" Ann just shrugged and inhaled deeply to light yet another cigarette.

The sound of a key on the lock made her jump to her feet and a moment later a distinguished-looking man in his sixties pushed open the sitting-room door. He was well dressed with a professional look about him and his

4

expression was grave.

"I just heard, Poppet," he said holding out his arms to Ann.

"She's missing Daddy . . . your little Moppet's missing," howled Ann, flinging herself into her father's arms and he patted her shoulders. Grace wondered how a man so obviously devoted to his daughter could leave her living alone in such a hostile environment with her child. She was clearly unable to cope.

After a moment Grace cleared her throat and Ann looked round. "Oh . . . sorry," she sniffed. "This is my father, Leonard Power." She disengaged herself. "Daddy, this is Detective Garda de Rossa, she's come about Moppet."

Leonard Power nodded gravely to Grace, then turning to Ann again said gently, "Go and make us a cup of tea, Poppet, there's a good girl." Ann meekly picked up the tea pot and padded towards the kitchen. Her father closed the door behind her.

"What do you think, Garda de Rossa, what do you think could have happened to my granddaughter?"

"We can't say at this time, Mr Power, do you think there's a possibility that she could have run away? I understand she was being bullied by the other kids."

Power drew his hands through his thin hair and sighed deeply, "I don't know."

"But you knew that she was being bullied?"

He looked down at the carpet. "Yes I knew . . . I should have made a stand . . . If I had, this would have never happened."

"Sorry?"

He sighed again and sat down heavily on the edge of an armchair. "Ann's mother. She disowned her when she got into trouble with Moppet . . . Nicolette. She wasn't married at the time you see . . . " he trailed off.

"But your daughter must have been in her late

5

twenties when she had Nicolette, surely her mother, your wife . . . "

Power interrupted her, "My wife is very religious, Miss de Rossa. What Ann did was against everything she believed in. She doesn't know that I support Ann and my granddaughter."

"What about the father? Do you think he may know where Nicolette is, do you think he might have her?"

Power looked astonished at her suggestion. "Absolutely not!"

"Why are you so positive ?"

He was thoughtful for a moment then said, "Because the father, whoever he is, certainly doesn't know of my granddaughter's existence."

The clattering of the china cups on a tray announced Ann's return.

"Would you mind if I take a look at Nicky's room, Ann?" Ann looked blankly back at her so Grace went on, "It may give us some hint of what's happened to her?"

Ann put down the tray. "Well yes . . . I suppose so." She led Grace up the stairs to the front bedroom. It was light and bright and pristine in keeping with the rest of Ann's home. A single bed with velvet headboard stood at right angles to the door, and under the window sat a pine dressing-table. The matching duvet cover and curtains were pastel pink as was the carpet, and the paintwork was sparkling white. A poster of a big-eyed fluffy puppy and a childlike clown with a single tear sitting on his cheek hung from the picture rail, and girlish bits and pieces were scattered round. A wicker chair in the corner of the room was piled high with soft toys and Grace was surprised that this childish room had been so recently occupied by a young teenager.

She wandered over to the wardrobe and opened it. "Are any of Nicky's clothes missing?"

Ann shambled over and listlessly ran her hand along

6

the row of hanging clothes; an empty hanger rattled to the floor. "It's hard to say . . . I can't see her jeans or her green sweat-shirt . . . "

"Are you all right?" Grace asked, seeing the older woman sway slightly as if she were going to fall.

Ann Power nodded. "Yes I'm fine . . . I took a couple of Valium just before you got here, I think they're beginning to work." She backed up and sat on the bed, once again wrapping her arms around her body and rocking. Grace was finding it unnerving.

"Her trainers have gone," Ann said suddenly, staring at the row of footwear lined up under the dressing-table, "and her schoolbag."

"Are you sure she wasn't wearing them when she left the house yesterday?" Ann Power just shrugged, her eyes were dead.

While rooting through the neatly folded underwear in the dressing-table, Grace found a small diary pushed to the back of the middle drawer. She flipped through the pages. Nicolette had minute slanted handwriting and each page was filled with a catalogue of each day's events. It was evident at the start of the year that the girl had suffered torments of bullying. It also seemed that her mother relied on her to do all the shopping, cleaning and cooking. Leonard Power featured on most pages.

"*Grampy collected me from school . . . Went for a drive with Grampy . . .* " But also one other name cropped up continually. "*Why does Philo Hoban hate me? . . . Philo dunked my head in the toilet . . . Gave Philo my homework to copy.*"

Further on she read, "*Philo is my friend at last, thank you God.*" And "*Went to Philo's after school, told Mother that I was at choir practice.*"

The sound of Leonard Power clearing his throat made Grace look up. "What's that?" he asked indicating the diary.

"It's Nicolette's diary, Mr Power. It seems she was friends with a girl called Philo Hoban. Does the name ring a bell?"

Power shook his head. "She never mentioned her." Then after a pause, "Do you think this girl may know where she is?"

"It's possible," said Grace holding up the diary. "May I borrow this?"

Power hesitated then said, "Whatever you need . . . may I look at it?" and almost grabbed the diary from her hand.

Grace turned to Ann who was still sitting passively on the bed. "Ann, how much money did Nicolette have with her when she left?"

Ann's speech was slightly slurred as she answered, "The housekeeping . . . about forty pounds I suppose." Then after a further pause she rushed on, "But she wouldn't leave me, someone's taken her . . . she wouldn't leave me."

Leonard Power sat down on the bed next to his daughter and put his arms round her. "Hush, Poppet, hush. I think Moppet may have run away for some reason, maybe because of this Hoban girl. But don't worry, we'll find her . . . we'll find her." Ann was sobbing into his shoulder. He looked up at Grace. "I'll take care of her Miss de Rossa." Handing the diary back to her he went on, "Take the diary if you think it will help."

Grace pulled the front door closed behind her. Ann and Leonard Power had left her feeling slightly depressed. One of the boys, having failed to demolish what was left of the wreck by jumping on it, was trying to bash in the side panel with an iron bar watched by the rest of the gang who, along with the negotiator, were leaning against the side of her car waiting for the second instalment. She handed over the money and they parted like the Red Sea, running off to spend it before the

8

bigger boys could bully them out of it.

She got lost again three times before she got off the estate and eventually headed towards the St Martin de Porres Community School. The playground was empty when she parked by the main entrance and the sound of children reciting French verbs, mingled with a slightly out of tune piano, drifted out from behind the windows closed against the chilly late March morning.

Sister Angela Mahon, the principal, politely answered her questions and denied any knowledge of specific bullying, but acknowledged that perhaps it might go on.

Nicolette Power didn't seem to have made much of an impression on her perhaps because she wasn't a troublemaker (Sister Angela's words.) But she gave Grace Philomena Hoban's address after informing her that the girl hadn't attended school for at least two weeks.

Nobody answered the door of number twenty James Larkin Tower but a neighbour told Grace that Nora Hoban would "be back after one and are youse her social worker?"

Grace headed back into the city and parked on a double yellow line in Clarendon Street. Her stomach was reminding her that she hadn't eaten since the previous evening and a late breakfast in Bewley's seemed a very appealing idea.

Grafton Street was bright and cheerful in the crisp spring sunshine and the feeling of gloom lifted as she walked down the paved pedestrian area past the opulent-looking shops. Though it was still quite early, a busker playing the violin had taken up a pitch near Marks & Spencer. She stood and listened for a few minutes to a piece of Vivaldi, throwing a pound into his hat.

Bewley's Oriental Café stands halfway down Grafton Street on the left as you walk from St Stephen's Green. It was opened at the end of the last century and was favoured by wits and writers, academics and students. The façade remains unchanged and the interior, although refurbished, maintains the same dignified air. Large art nouveau stained glass panels designed by Harry Clarke are set high into the rear walls.

The café was crowded as usual and the hum of conversation echoed off the high ceilings. As she waited in line to get her breakfast fry, the aroma of freshly ground coffee and frying bacon rashers teased her taste buds. A table by the big open fire caught her eye and she circumnavigated two large middle-aged housewives to reach it first. They glared and tut-tutted to her back but she plonked her tray down and spread her breakfast out, smiling to herself. After attacking the rashers, white pudding and scrambled eggs, she settled back with her coffee to read Nicky's diary in more detail.

Nicky had found her protector towards the middle of January, though, apart from allowing the girl to copy her homework, Grace couldn't see any reason why Philo had so suddenly changed her tune towards the unfortunate Nicolette. She could sense Philo's influence growing in the following pages and an element of rebellion in criticisms of Ann Power which started to creep in, usually preceded by "Philo says" or "Philo thinks".

"February 2nd: Mother was worse than ever today, she hadn't even washed up the breakfast dishes when I got home from school. She was doped out of it. I yelled at her and she started to cry again. Grampy says I have to be patient.

February 3rd: Grampy was annoyed when I didn't want to go for a drive after school. Mother was as bad when I got home late, I wish they would leave me alone. Philo says I should stand up to them.

February 4th: Went to Video Paradise with . . . "

"Grace! . . . listen dear, that whore's pregnant, can you believe it?" Kathleen flounced down at her table all ruffled feathers, Estée Lauder and Switzer's bags.

Grace winced. When Andrew, her husband of eight years had moved out six months before, she hadn't exactly been heartbroken. Humiliated, betrayed maybe, but the marriage had been dead on its feet anyway. The betrayal by Kiera Lyons, her friend since childhood, had been more of an upset, but she was coming to terms with that. What she hadn't expected was to lose her husband only to retain her mother-in-law. Kathleen Dillon was an attractive, striking woman of fifty-five. She had been widowed at a young age but left very well off by her late husband. Grace had married her only son Andrew, much to the delight of Grace's own mother, Alice, who had been Kathleen's best friend for decades. Alice also felt that by marrying a solicitor, Grace had redeemed herself from the shame and disappointment she had caused by not following her siblings into the medical profession.

"Hello Kathleen. Nice to see you," Grace said trying to sound sincere. Kathleen leaned over the table and they both kissed air. "You know I really don't care. I don't know why you're bothering to tell me this."

Kathleen took her hand and patting the back said, "You're still in denial, dear, of course you care . . . but don't you worry, she's a trollop . . . he'll soon see through . . . "

"Kathleen please, I really *really* don't care. Kiera can have him." She half stood and started to gather her things together. "Look, you'll have to excuse me, I have to be somewhere."

Not to be put off, Kathleen still held on grimly to her daughter-in-law's hand. "You poor dear. You shouldn't blame Andrew, he'll come to his senses," she said and Grace thought she saw the ghost of a tear in the older woman's eye.

It took Grace a further five minutes to extricate herself from Kathleen's vice-like grip and they kissed air again before she fled back into Grafton Street with

11

empty promises of meeting for lunch sometime.

Back at the office in Harcourt Terrace she sat at her desk and took the diary out of her bag again.

"February 4th: Went to Video Paradise with Philo. She knows everyone."

The daily entries continued in this vein, and abruptly stopped three weeks before, on March the first.

"March 1st: Met Kevo and Anto again. Anto fancies me. Grampy would be livid if I told him!"

"Did you see Mrs Power?" asked Hatchett, who was passing through the room on the way to lunch. Grace looked up. "Yes . . . " she said absently.

"And?"

"And I'm not sure. I think that the girl's probably a runaway . . . though I'm not sure yet. I have to see a friend of hers at one."

"OK. Try and wind it up as quick as you can, will you? I'm sorry I had to get you out early but Hugh O'Boyle, Jack Mulloy and Kate O'Grady all called in sick, so I'd no choice."

Hatchett's uncharacteristic solicitous remark knocked Grace off balance. "No problem," she said, feeling guilty about the uncharitable thoughts she had harboured about her boss earlier that morning.

Nora Hoban was expecting her social worker and was more than a little disappointed when Grace showed her her warrant card.

"What d'you want then?" she demanded.

"I wanted to see your daughter Philomena."

"Why . . . What's she done?" asked Nora looking wary.

"Nothing that I know of," said Grace smiling. "Do you know Nicky Power?"

Relieved that her daughter wasn't in any kind of trouble, Nora said, "Yes, she's a pal of Philo's. She's been here a couple of times . . . nice polite kid. What d'yez want her for, she doesn't seem like the sort yez normally want to talk to?"

"She's gone missing. Would Philo have any notion where she could be?"

Nora shrugged. "Yez'd have to ask her that yerself. Would yez like a cup of tea?"

"No thanks, Nora. Where is Philomena?"

Nora threw back her head and snorted. "The little whooer buggered off with the rent money an' me bingo winnin's a week ago . . . I thought yez were goin' to say yez'd picked her up for shopliftin' or somethin'." Then she gave a throaty laugh.

"Do you think she and Nicky could be together?"

"Maybe."

Grace tried a different tack. "Do you know a couple of lads called Anto and Kevo?"

Nora shook her head and shrugged. "Half the kids round here are called Anto or Kevo or Tommo."

"If you don't mind me saying so," said Grace after a moment, "you don't seem very worried about Phil."

Nora snorted again, "She's streetwise that one. She'll be back when she's spent all me money."

"Do you have a recent photo of Philo I could borrow?" Grace asked, and Nora went into the flat to get one. As she was standing on the landing waiting, a young girl wandered round the corner from the lifts. She stopped dead at the sight of Grace and looked her up and down suspiciously.

Just then Nora returned with the picture and seeing the girl screamed, "Get in here, yeh little whooer" and shook her fists. The girl turned tail and pelted back to the lifts. "That's her . . . that's my Philo, the little bastard," Nora roared, and Grace set off in hot pursuit reaching the lifts just as the doors closed.

Nora gave her the photo in exchange for a promise that Grace would give the little bitch a clip round the ear if she caught up with her.

Chapter Two

Surveillance is probably the next most boring activity after watching paint dry.

Two days before Leonard Power had called on Grace at Harcourt Terrace to show her a postcard with a Dublin postmark that he had received from his granddaughter, stating that she was safe and well and not to worry about her. It seemed a bit pat to Grace but she compared it to the handwriting in the girl's diary before handing it back to Power. The card looked authentic.

Dermot McEvoy and Grace were sitting in an unmarked car waiting for the evening shift to take over from them. It was dusk, the day was cold and miserable and the McDowell brothers hadn't moved out of the house all day. She could see them sitting in the warmth and comfort of their well-lit, well-heated sitting-room and she felt pangs of envy.

Detective Sergeant Dermot McEvoy had been a member of the gardaí for twenty-five years, most of it spent in and around the capital. He was a widower with three daughters, all just about grown-up. Grace had learnt a lot about police work from him in the four years that they had worked together. He had a volatile temperament but she sometimes found his attitude a touch jaded, even a little callous, a fact she put down to the number of years he had been in the job.

A black BMW swung into the driveway and she aimed the camera and took several frames of the car and the occupant before he entered the house.

"Who's that?" Dermot asked.

"It looks like Brawn, the solicitor."

They sat and lapsed into silence again, watching as the evening traffic swished past through the rain.

"This is a waste of time. I can't see them bringing the videos here, can you?"

"Ours is not to reason why," said Dermot. "That's the information that Eugene Flynn, the little shit, gave me. Who knows? Maybe we'll get lucky."

"Maybe pigs will fly."

"An unfortunate choice of words if I may say so," said Dermot and Grace smiled suddenly.

Branden and Alan McDowell were making every effort to emulate the Kray twins. They came from humble beginnings in Donore Avenue and now lived in one of two adjoining Georgian properties which they owned outright in prestigious Wellington Road. The second building housed the offices of their security company, Feel Safe Security, and it was common knowledge that this was a not very subtle cover for their protection racket. Their rise to prominence had been swift, brought about by wiping out the opposition by any means possible, and they had diversified into many other almost legitimate areas including hot dog stands, snooker clubs and video rentals.

The information received concerned a shipment of bootleg videos smuggled in from Holland the previous week to be delivered to Feel Safe Security. Other units were watching the video rental outlets and snooker clubs in case there was any change of plan.

Hugh O'Boyle slid into the back seat and the rush of cold air that followed him made Grace shiver.

"How's it goin'?" he said by way of a greeting.

"Not much movement," said Grace. "The solicitor went in about ten minutes ago."

"That's handy. If you ask me this is a fuckin' waste of time. Wouldn't be surprised if they'd planted the information just to keep us occupied." As he spoke a Hiace van pulled into the drive in front of Feel Safe Security. As the driver got out, three men hurried down the steps out of the building.

"On the other hand, maybe not," said Grace.

Dermot got on the radio. "Looks like a go, lads. There's a Hiace about to unload outside Feel Safe."

As the men started to unload cardboard packing cases, three unmarked garda cars screeched to a halt blocking both driveways. Grace, Dermot, Hugh and five other members of the unit piled out of their vehicles. The three men, who by this time were pinned to the side of the Hiace by three of the unit, were cursing and shouting and the driver had run up the adjacent steps and was banging on the front door of McDowells' house.

Grace ripped open one of the cartons. Empty plastic video rental cases spilled out onto the tarmac. She tried four other cartons at random with the same result. Light flooded down the steps as the front door opened.

"Is there a problem, Sergeant McEvoy?" Branden McDowell, with his legal representative at his side, stood framed in the doorway, looking down at Dermot with a broad grin on his face. The whole unit knew that they had just been had.

Later in Smyths, Grace nursed a hot whiskey and Dermot a Smithwicks, as they sat in a state bordering on depression. The pub was jammed with early evening drinkers and everyone else seemed to be in good humour.

"Shit!" said Dermot suddenly as he saw Jack Staunton and Geoff Murphy from the drug squad pushing their way through the throng to join them. They stood beside

Grace's stool and talked together as if neither she nor Dermot were there.

"It's not April the first, is it Jack?"

"No, Geoff, It's not April the first. Why d'you ask?"

"Well, Jack, I heard that the lads from Harcourt Terrace are going to be on Beadle's About."

"Go on, Murphy, twist the knife," said Grace. "May the road rise up to meet you and may you fall down a deep sewer!"

"Jesus, but that was bad luck, lads," said Jack. "Were ye set up or what?"

"I think it was a case of or what," said Dermot. "Though Eugene Flynn'll wish for death when I catch up with him."

"Was it Flynn?" asked Geoff. "That little prat was busted for possession this morning, he's on remand in Mountjoy right now."

Grace shot a look at Dermot and the two of them knocked back their drinks. "Thank you gentlemen," she said over her shoulder as they hurried out of the door.

Flynn, who had a serious drug habit, was sweating profusely and had a bad case of the shakes by the time they got to see him. He was sitting huddled over a table in the interview room, sniffing and wiping his dripping nose on his shirt sleeve.

"Thanks be to God, Mr McEvoy," he said as soon as he saw Dermot. He jumped to his feet. "I knew you wouldn't let me down."

"Pity I can't say the same about you, Eugene."

"Wha'?" he said looking surprised. "I look after you, don't I? I give you good stuff . . . I gave you the McDowells didn't I?"

"No, Eugene, you didn't," said Grace. "You made us look a like a crowd of eejits. Now what's the story?"

Eugene looked at Grace. "What d'you mean . . . didn't you get the videos?"

17

"There were no bent videos, Eugene, but you know that already don't you?" As he spoke Dermot punctuated each word with a push to Eugene's shoulder. Eugene ended up squashed up against the wall, his face inches from Dermot's. "We don't like spending two days sitting in a fucking freezing cold car and being made to look fucking eejits at the end of it . . . do we Garda de Rossa."

"I don't know what you're talkin' about. On my kids' lives, Mr McEvoy . . . on my kids' lives. If anythin' went wrong it had to be at your end. I swear."

"Nice try, Eugene," said Grace. "But just remember your card's marked."

"Look . . . it's not like that, what I told you was a hundred per fuckin' cent." Suddenly a thought seemed to strike Eugene with the force of a two ton truck. "Jesus! Mr McEvoy you've got to look after me . . . Them McDowells are animals . . . they'll know I grassed them up . . . I'm fuckin' dead meat when they get to me . . . You've got to help me." Terror contorted his features, tears started to run down his cheeks and he was clinging tightly onto Dermot's lapels.

Dermot peeled the grubby hands free and pushed him down on to the chair.

"One way or another you're finished then, aren't you Flynn?" said Grace. "Come on, Dermot, let's get out of here, if I wanted a fairy tale I'd have gone to see Snow White . . . "

As the door closed behind them they could still hear Flynn shouting the odds.

Dermot dropped Grace at the car park and she drove on home. She needed a long soak in a hot bath to wash away the smell of Mountjoy and was just about to slide under the perfumed bubbles when there was a ring at the front door. Cursing to herself, she grabbed her dressing-gown and went down to answer it. Andrew was standing on the doorstep.

"Hello Grace, I wonder if I could have a word?" She stood staring at him so he walked past her along the hall and into the kitchen. "I didn't like to use my key. I haven't come at a bad time have I?"

Grace closed the front door and followed him into the kitchen. She hadn't laid eyes on him for four months and here he was chatting on as if nothing had happened.

He leaned against the edge of the kitchen table with his hands in his pockets, he looked relaxed and at ease. "It was quite cold today . . . "

"Andrew . . . What do you want?" she said mystified. "I'm sure you didn't come here just to discuss the bloody weather."

"Well no. We, Kiera and I, need a bigger place and we thought that it would be a good idea if we did a swop with you."

"What?" was all she managed to say, anger rising in her chest.

"It's quite simple really. If you were to buy Kiera's house in Gray Street and she bought your share of this house, it would save all of us a lot of bother not to mention expense . . . that's all really," he added lamely seeing her thunderous expression.

"Oh is that all! She wants to steal my house from under me as well as my husband."

"Come on Grace . . . You know it's not like that." That was the straw that broke the camel's back. That and the accumulation of the day's events made Grace boil over. Andrew was as good a person to vent her spleen on as any.

"Of course it's exactly like that! Don't I get a say in this? Don't my wishes count for anything in this?" she screamed. "You think you can waltz in here and sell my house from under me just so you and that bitch can have an extra room for the nursery . . . "

Andrew stood placidly where he was. It was like

arguing with a bowl of water. "So that's what this hysteria is about," he said without raising his voice. "You're jealous because we're going to have a child."

"Get real, Andrew, since when did you ever want a child?"

He looked hurt. "I've always wanted children."

"Liar!" she spat. "Since when? Whenever anyone asks you if you like children your stock answer's always 'not enough to eat a whole one'. Who the hell are you trying to kid?"

The only visible sign of irritation showing in Andrew's body language was a slight tightening of his jaw. "Don't be childish, Grace."

They stood in silence, toe to toe, Grace fumed. Andrew just stared at her, waiting for her to say something.

Eventually, feeling stupid and humiliated, she tried to salvage what was left of her dignity by saying, "I'll get my solicitor to write to you." And turning on her heel, she headed back toward the stairs.

"Is that a yes or a no?"

"Close the door on your way out," she said from half a flight up. And as he closed the door quietly behind him, she sat on the top step of the stairs and started to cry. Only then did she remember that *he* was her solicitor.

Chapter Three

There's nothing quite like a good cry, a hot soak and a good night's sleep to make the world feel like a better place, even when it isn't. Grace wandered down Grafton Street, window-shopping. It was her day off, the sun was shining and the street was crowded with shoppers, buskers and people just hanging out. She stood for a while on the edge of a crowd and watched a couple of mime artists, but then, bored with that, strolled off again.

A pair of ridiculously high, stupendously expensive, bright red Italian shoes caught her eye in Carl Scarpa's window. She argued with herself before finally relenting and going in to try them on. They were impossible to walk in and she had nothing to go with them but she bought them anyway, for therapeutic reasons she rationalised later, over a cup of cappuccino with her sister Faith.

"What's the crisis?" Faith asked after examining the new shoes, eyeing the large piece of lemon cheesecake on Grace's plate. Grace told her about the previous day's fiasco, of Andrew's visit and of the total fool she had made of herself.

Faith, at thirty-two, was two years younger than Grace and had fulfilled their parents' expectations by qualifying as a gynaecologist, marrying a consultant neurosurgeon, and producing three children in the meantime. Of her four sisters and two brothers, Faith was the one with whom she got on the best despite their totally different lifestyles and aspirations. Grace and Faith also resembled each other more than the rest of the family. They were both taller than average with copper-coloured hair, pale skin and high cheekbones. They had athletic bodies, though Faith's had thickened round the waist somewhat after her three babies were born within the first four years of her marriage.

It had been she who had soothed Grace's battered ego when Andrew had left, pointing out to Grace the fact that her weeping and gnashing of teeth had been self-pity and humiliation rather than sorrow, and that the relationship was long dead anyway.

They sat together at a window table in the coffee shop looking out into Crown Alley. The narrow cobbled street was part of the Temple Bar area of the city. For years Temple Bar had fallen into decay, but the old buildings were being renovated and gentrified and the area was buzzing back to life with second-hand clothes shops, restaurants and pubs.

"I never liked him," Fay commented. "He never was the most sensitive of souls, your Andrew. And trying to uproot you as well. As if running off with your best friend wasn't bad enough."

"I know what you mean," said Grace gravely. "And I really miss her!" Faith, in mid-swallow, choked on her cappuccino.

Grace thumped her on the back. "And you know what the worst part is?"

"What?" asked her sister, still coughing and wiping flecks of froth off a perfect Armani lapel.

"Swapping houses is actually quite a good idea."

Faith looked dubious. "I don't think you've thought this through, Grace. Where is Kiera's house anyway?"

"Gray Street . . . that's just off Meath Street," said

Grace. Faith grimaced. "Oh don't be such a snob, Fay . . . it's a cute little house."

"*Cute!* . . . Cute is not the best criterion to use when buying a home, Grace. Good resale value, excellent repair, nice area, good state of decoration maybe, those are the attributes that spring to mind . . . But cute . . . and Meath Street to boot. There are still hostile natives roaming about there!"

Faith was beginning to irritate Grace. "You sound like Father," she said. "I can just imagine him wringing his hands and telling Mother how I've disgraced the family again. I might just move for spite, just to see if he gets round mentioning to his friends that his black sheep daughter's moved to the inner city, and the Liberties to boot." She spooned the froth from her coffee, enjoying the thought of her father's discomfort, but the feeling didn't last long. She looked across the table at Faith and added, "Anyway I haven't the time or the energy to hunt for anything else."

"Well stay put then, I don't see why you should have to move in the first place." They lapsed into silence, Faith tapped her saucer with the teaspoon, jaw set and Grace stared out of the window.

Two youths were arguing with each on the opposite pavement, a traffic warden was ignoring the protests of a young woman with red dreadlocks and a child balanced on one hip, who had parked her old battered Renault half-on, half-off the kerb on the double yellow lines. Faith started to lay down the law again but Grace wasn't listening. She'd caught sight of a familiar face. Leaning against a bollard, looking a good deal older than her fourteen years, was Philo Hoban. Grace jumped up and leaving Faith in mid-sentence said over her shoulder, "I'll be back in a minute."

By the time she reached the pavement Philo had disappeared. Grace looked up and down Crown Alley and saw Philo turning into Temple Bar. She took off after her and caught up with her at the corner of Fleet Street. Philo appeared to be waiting for something.

"Philo Hoban?"

The girl looked at her suspiciously. "Why?"

Grace smiled at her, trying to put her at ease. "Hello, Philo, my name's Grace, I was looking for Nicolette Power. Do you know where she is?"

Philo still looked wary. "I saw you at me ma's . . . Why're you askin' me, how should I know?"

"Look Philo, I know you were friendly with her. If she's with you it's OK, but her mother and grandfather are very worried about her."

Philo stared at her as if trying to make up her mind whether to talk to her or not. Finally she said, "You a social worker or somethin'?"

"No," said Grace.

Again Philo was silent. Close up she looked very much her age, even the lycra mini and heavy make-up couldn't hide the fact that she was only just past being a child.

"You're a guard, righ'?" When Grace didn't answer she went on to say, "She did it then . . . she hopped it?"

"I don't know for sure . . . was she talking about it?"

Philo frowned. "A bit. I felt sorry for her . . . I told her she didn't have to put up with it. Maybe she listened to me."

"Put up with what?" asked Grace.

The girl shrugged and cast her eyes down again. Grace repeated the question and after what seemed like an age Philo said, "You know . . . her ma . . . the auld fella. She had her doin' everythin', and he was messin' with her."

Grace was stunned. "What do you mean messing?" she asked, having a very good idea what she did mean.

"You know, messin'," Philo said looking uncomfortable. "Interferin' with her."

24

"Philo, think carefully before you answer. Did Nicky actually tell you that her grandfather was sexually abusing her?" said Grace, holding Philo by the shoulders to emphasise the seriousness of the question. "Did she actually tell you that?"

Philo shrugged free. "Yeh . . . kind of . . . she didn't know that it wasn't right till I put her straight, but she didn't like it. She wanted him to stop."

"Do you know where she is?" Grace asked, not wanting to let the girl go.

"No . . . How would I know where she'd go?"

Grace didn't believe her. "Come on, Philo, Nicky wouldn't know what to do or where to go, she's not streetwise like you are." The girl drew back from her and Grace realised that she was grasping her shoulders again. Philo stared up at Grace and was about to speak, then changed her mind. "Come on Philo, this is important," Grace urged, she was beginning to lose her patience. Abruptly the girl pushed past her but she grabbed her arm. "Please Philo . . . If you know where Nicky is I can help her, you know she'll never survive on the streets."

Philo shrugged free. "I don't know where she is but I'll ask around . . . now I have to go, I'm goin' to be in a film." She pronounced the word fill-um.

Grace rooted in her bag and pulled out a card. "Here's my number, phone me if you hear anything. By the way does your mother know where you are?"

"Fuck off," said the woman-child and darted off into the crowd. Grace saw her jump into the back of a red Passat further down the street and speed off towards the centre of the city.

By the time she got back to the coffee shop Faith was just coming out. "Sorry Fay," she said, out of breath. "I saw someone I had to talk to."

Faith gave her an old-fashioned look and handed her the bag containing the shoes. "You ought to be talking to a solicitor, and I don't mean Andrew. Now promise me you will." Grace promised her sister that she would do as she asked and they kissed and went their separate ways.

On her way back home she stopped off at Harcourt Terrace to see if Inspector Hatchett was in. She wasn't sure what action to take, if any, on the information Philo had given her, and didn't even know whether to believe her or not either.

"Are you still convinced that she's a runaway?" Hatchett asked her.

"I think so. And I have to ask myself *why*, if she is. If what Philo Hoban claims is true, it would be a good enough reason."

"Is there a social worker?"

Grace shook her head. "No. The mother keeps to herself, they're not a problem family on the face of it. Not claiming welfare or anything. The grandfather supports them, unbeknown to his wife from what I can gather. It's kind of a strange set-up."

"And there's still no sign of the girl?"

"No, sir."

Hatchett swung from side to side in his swivel chair, hands clasped loosely in his lap. "Then I don't see what we can do at the moment. We've no victim . . . no complainant, just a runaway fourteen-year-old of dubious credibility making unfounded accusations."

"I know . . . but it doesn't feel right. Should I talk to Leonard Power again, see how he reacts?"

"I suppose you could, but what do you think he's going to say? Even if what the Hoban girl says is true. He's hardly going to put his hands up to it, is he?" Grace didn't comment. "No, on second thoughts," said Hatchett, "leave well enough alone and when the girl turns up, talk to her about it."

At five-fifty the following morning Grace ran down the

26

steps of Harcourt Terrace Garda Station and bumped into Dermot on his way in. "They just pulled Eugene Flynn out of the Liffey," she said. "They've taken him to James's."

Dermot turned and followed her. "Is he dead?"

"Very dead. Pretty badly beaten too apparently, both arms broken."

"What d'you think?" he said. "The McDowells?"

Grace had had the same thought. "I hope not. If it is then it's our fault. The poor bastard, maybe we should have listened to him."

"Bullshit!"

They drove in silence, the roads were quiet due to the early hour and they reached the hospital fifteen minutes later.

"You know, Grace, it's probably nothing to do with the McDowells, it could be drug-related, anything. He wasn't the most well-liked person in the universe. I wouldn't waste your sympathy, he was just a piece of garbage." Grace didn't comment as they made their way to the morgue, she was trying to ignore her strong feelings of guilt, without much success.

A couple of detective gardaí from Store Street, whom Grace only knew by sight, were leaning against the wall outside the morgue. Flynn had been taken from the river by the North Wall so they were dealing with the incident. They stopped talking when they saw Grace and Dermot approaching and nodded a greeting.

"D'you mind if we take a look, Paul," said Dermot to the elder of the two men.

"Help yourself," he said indicating the swing doors. "What's your interest?"

"He was an informant of mine," said Dermot.

"Stands to reason," said Byrne.

Grace stopped halfway through the door. "Why d'you say that?"

He sniffed and looked at his partner, then back at Grace. "His tongue's been cut out."

"Christ!"

That was the least of Eugene Flynn's worries. Laid out on the mortuary table in the glaring light reflected off the floor to ceiling tiles, his drug-wasted frame looked even more pathetic than it did in life. The torso was black and blue with the marks of what looked like a baseball bat. His once skinny arms were covered with needle marks. His face was barely recognisable, the nose was smashed and both eyes closed, blackened and bloody. "Useless looking article, isn't he," said Dermot, standing impassively with his hands in his pockets.

"Sometimes, Dermot, you can be such a shit," hissed Grace. "He was a human being."

"Just about," was his reply as he lifted up Flynn's lifeless hand and examined the fingers through the plastic bag that encased them. "They ripped out his fingernails too, look."

Grace looked over his shoulder and wrinkled her nose. "It goes to prove that there are worse things in life than death," she said. "I'd say he was begging to be put out of it by the time the animals who did this had finished. Poor sod."

They heard the doors swing open and Paul Byrne wandered in. He stood behind Grace and the three of them stared at the late Eugene Flynn in silence. After about half a minute Byrne said, "Occupational hazard I suppose . . . bit over the top though."

"I suppose they were trying to make a point," said Grace. "Though sticking his head on the railings of Dublin Castle would have been a touch more subtle."

"I doubt that subtlety is their forte," said Dermot.

"And who do you think *they* are?" asked Byrne.

"The McDowell brothers," Dermot and Grace said in unison.

"Would I be right in thinking this has something to do with your unfortunate incident the other day?"

"It was Flynn who grassed on the McDowells, though after the event we thought he'd set us up, poor bastard," Grace said with genuine regret.

"So who grassed Flynn up then?"

"It could have been anyone," said Dermot sardonically. "He was an addict and a loser . . . he probably blabbed to half of Dublin when he was high."

"I won't hold my breath waiting for witnesses to come forward then," said Byrne stating the obvious. "When the gory details get out I'd say they'll be pretty thin on the ground."

"I wonder what was the actual cause of death?" said Grace to no one in particular.

"Take your pick," volunteered Byrne. "There'll be three or four to choose from after the post-mortem, but if the McDowells are the technicians I think they are, he probably drowned."

After driving for ten minutes in silence on the return journey to Harcourt Terrace, Dermot suddenly said, "I wouldn't bother feeling guilty about Flynn, Grace. He was a loser, he knew what he was into and would have sold you out just as quickly if it suited him for the price of a fix."

"That's not the point," Grace answered irritably. "Nobody deserves to go through what he did. And don't forget he had a wife and kids."

"Granted . . . but I still wouldn't waste my sympathy. As for the wife and kids, they'll be better off without him." They completed the journey in a slightly frosty silence.

Halfway through the morning Hatchett called Dermot into his office and when he returned ten minutes later he was in a foul humour. "Branden bloody McDowell's lodged a formal complaint against me for harassment," he said. "Can you credit that?" Grace burst out laughing, more at Dermot's expression of utter frustration and incredulity than anything else.

"Well I'm glad you find it so funny," he snapped. "They're making common eejits out of all of us and all you morons can do is make a joke out of it." That said, he turned and stormed out of the office slamming the door.

Grace looked over at Jack Mulloy and grimaced, and still laughing said, "Ooops! . . . What is it with him and the McDowells?"

"Don't you know?" said Jack, looking up from his newspaper.

"Know what?"

"Dermot's wife was killed by a hit-and-run driver twelve years ago."

"I know . . . So?"

"So, did you know that the car was Branden McDowell's, and that he had it reported stolen and had an alibi fixed up well before he was even lifted."

Chapter Four

Phoebe Lamplighter sat stiffly in her chair. She was a dark, good-looking woman in her early forties, well groomed, expensively dressed, well spoken and very well preserved.

"Where did you get the credit card, Phoebe?"

Phoebe lit a long brown cigarette and blew the smoke up to the ceiling. "I told you already, I found it," she snapped. "How many more times do I have to say it? I didn't steal the card, I found it and I was about to hand it in at a garda station when that moron kicked off."

"That moron" was Phoebe's last client, a middle-aged business man up from the country who was downstairs with Jack Mulloy, ranting and raving about his lost wallet. The stolen credit card had come to light quite by accident after the newly introduced client, the worse for drink, had created a scene in the plush hotel bar where he had rendezvoused with Phoebe, claiming that she had stolen it. After the gardaí had been called and Phoebe had been arrested, the gold Visa card in the name of Veronica Hyde had been found in her bag, though there was no sign of the missing property.

"What about the punter's wallet?"

"God! I don't need this hassle," Phoebe said suddenly, losing her composure for the first time. "The stupid prat just lost it . . . I'm not a thief."

"Just a whore . . . " commented Hugh O'Boyle under his breath.

Phoebe glared at him. "Watch your mouth, O'Boyle, you can't prove I stole the credit card and I'm sure when that eejit downstairs sobers up he'll realise that his little wife in Ballywherever won't be too thrilled at the implications of a court case."

Grace shrugged. "If the prosecution persuades the jury that you were involved in the mugging you're talking prison."

"What mugging? . . . What are you talking about?" Phoebe sounded alarmed.

"The owner of the card was attacked, her leg was broken . . . "

"We can do you for being a common prostitute anyway," Hugh cut in. "Even without the Visa card . . . That should put a halt to your gallop."

"I run a legitimate escort service, you can't prove otherwise," Phoebe fumed.

"Well the publicity of a court appearance won't do your legitimate business a lot of good then, will it?" Hugh said grinning.

"What *is* it with you? Why can't you just leave me alone? I'm not doing you any harm," she said stubbing out her cigarette vigorously in the ashtray. "What do you want from me?"

"Just the name of the person running the credit card scam . . . that'll do for starters."

Phoebe sat staring at the table top, she looked worried. The last thing she needed was the bad publicity of a court appearance; her very lucrative business depended on discretion above all else.

Phoebe Lamplighter had been born in Galway city of strict, well-off middle-class parents. Always ambitious, she had moved to Dublin at the age of eighteen to do a secretarial course and from there to New York. She soon became discontent with the meagre lifestyle office jobs afforded and was persuaded by a friend to join an escort agency. Phoebe soon realised that she could earn a lot more money supplying extra services over and above escort duty to her clients, and after six months she gave up the day job and started to make plans. Two years later, with financial help from a client, she opened her own upmarket agency and started to make a lot more money with the added benefit of not having to earn her living flat on her own back.

Life was sweet. She rented plush offices on the Upper West Side complete with penthouse apartment, drank only champagne and wore imported designer clothes. Discretion was the agency's watchword and new clients were introduced on the personal recommendation of existing trusted patrons. All went well for ten years until a local politician with a monster grudge for some long forgotten slight had her convicted of keeping a bawdy house and abruptly deported as an illegal alien.

She returned home almost penniless, nearly all her funds having been confiscated or frozen by the authorities. Life was suddenly not so sweet anymore.

She had tenaciously struggled and pulled herself up by her bootlaces to establish another business, using all her past experience and expertise, albeit on a much smaller scale than the New York operation, and now sitting in the dingy interview room she could see it slipping away because of one stupid mistake. I'll kill bloody Martin Kennedy for vouching for that prat! she thought to herself, cursing that she had broken her own rules and not checked up on him.

Grace sat staring at her; she had never met Phoebe before and she certainly didn't fit the stereotype of the oldest profession.

Phoebe reached into her handbag for another cigarette trying to look unconcerned but Grace could sense her anxiety.

"Well . . . ?" prompted Grace. "Who's running the bent credit cards, Phoebe?"

The older woman stared steadily back, nervously tapping her fingernail on the table-top. After a while she said, "Watch my lips . . . I don't know anything about bent credit cards."

Hugh gave an exaggerated sigh. "Suit yourself," he said and got up from the table and walked towards the door. "D'you want to call a brief before you're charged?"

"Charged! . . . Wait . . . What if I could give you some information about something else?" Phoebe reached out and grabbed his arm.

Hugh stopped. "What information?"

She relaxed a little. "Something that could put the McDowell brothers away," she said nonchalantly trying not to look smug.

Grace shot a look at Hugh who was still half out of the door. "That would depend," she said. "We couldn't make any promises. What's this information?"

Phoebe burst out laughing. "Oh no . . . nothing until I'm on a promise," she said, and Grace went to look for Dermot leaving Hugh with Phoebe. She fervently hoped that she really had kosher stuff on the McDowells so that Dermot could get them out of his system for once and for all.

She found him in the canteen and his eyes lit up briefly when she told him someone was prepared to seriously grass up his *bête noire*, but he soon regained his usual cynicism when she told him who the informant was. He guffawed loudly.

"Well at least come and listen to what she has to say," Grace said irritably. "What've you got to lose."

"I believe you want to talk to me?" he said to Phoebe when they entered the room.

"That would depend on what you can offer me," Phoebe replied.

34

Dermot shrugged. "Did you use the bent Visa yet?"

"I didn't steal the Visa card, I was going to hand it in."

"That's not what I asked," snapped Dermot. "I said did you *use* it."

Phoebe pursed her lips. "*No I did not,*" she said, slowly pronouncing the words as if she were addressing a small child. "And if you don't want to put the McDowells away, then sod you."

Dermot sat down on the edge of the table and said nothing for a while as he stared at the wall. Abruptly he stood and said, "OK. If you have something on the McDowells that we can use, Garda O'Boyle won't bring charges against you, but if you're giving us so much bullshit I'll have you back here so fast your feet won't touch the ground."

Phoebe gave him a sweet smile. "Thank you so much," she replied, not without sarcasm. Then, "The McDowells are branching out. They're running kids."

"What d'you mean?" Grace asked.

"Kids. They're pimping for kids . . . forcing them to turn tricks."

"And . . . ?" Dermot said impatiently.

"What do you mean *and*? . . . They're selling kids for God's sake, what more do you want on them?"

"Proof," Hugh replied. "Hearsay isn't good enough."

Phoebe shrugged. "OK . . . Tomorrow night Branden McDowell's shooting a video of three kids in a warehouse in Ringsend . . . a sort of mail order video catalogue, if you know what I mean . . . "

"How d'you know this?"

"Because Seán Platt, the guy they have shooting the epic, asked me to help . . . I told him I wasn't interested."

"Presumably this video will be blue in nature?" Dermot said sounding interested for the first time, but Phoebe Lamplighter just cast her large green eyes heavenwards. "What do you think?" she said flatly.

Hatchett was unimpressed with Phoebe. "She's a whore, isn't she?" he said when Grace filled him in.

"Well yes . . . " Grace said, irritated by his attitude. "But that doesn't mean she's automatically lying, does it?"

"We'll see," he said pointedly, and reluctantly agreed to sanction a surveillance operation for the following day.

Much later Grace went off duty for the day and decided to have a night in, not that that was much of a change for her. Her social life had dwindled to nothing since Andrew had flown the coop, most of their joint friends found the situation more than a little awkward and addressed the problem by designating Andrew and Kiera as a couple and pretending that she didn't exist.

She stopped at the video shop on her way home and scanned the shelves for something light and funny to take her mind of her problems, and picked up a six pack and a take-away to save having to make a decision about what to cook. The take-away gave her someone else's order and the video in the Steve Martin cover was a weepy terminal illness movie, but apart from that the evening was OK.

At about ten-thirty, when she was ready to start on her second box of tissues and the child with kidney failure was about to die for lack of a transplant the doorbell rang. Kiera was standing on the doorstep. Grace hadn't seen her since she and Andrew had rearranged her marital status.

"Hello Grace," was all she said. She stood waiting for Grace to respond. Grace stared at her and eventually the ensuing silence prompted Kiera to say, "Aren't you going to ask me in, it's cold out here?"

"No," said Grace. "What d'you want? . . . Come to measure up for the curtains have you?"

"Don't be like that Grace." Kiera walked past her into the hall. "I expect you're wondering what I'm doing here."

"We already established that, Kiera. You've come to measure up for curtains and to explain the merits of your little house-swapping scheme as opposed to your wife-swapping scheme."

"Well no actually . . . I wanted to apologise for everything that's happened and ask you if we could still be friends . . . "

Grace, who was still standing stunned by the open front door shook her head vigorously from side to side and snapped, "You've got to be out of your mind . . . I'd rather push my nose into the electric can-opener."

"No . . . Look, don't be like that. I know you were hurt, but Andrew and I fell in love, we couldn't help it, it just happened like that."

"I don't think you quite grasp what I'm angry about, Kiera. It's not the fact that you and my husband chose to fall in love, it was the deceit, that you both lied to me . . . and I was the last to know, but then I suppose that's always the case, isn't it? The wife's always the last to know."

Kiera, from looking cowed, suddenly looked furious. "What the hell did you expect? You neglected him. He may as well have been single for all the time the two of you spent together, no wonder all our friends look on us as a couple, we've been that way for long enough."

Grace had to concede this point. Kiera and Andrew had often attended functions together when Grace was working or just didn't feel like going. In a way she'd pushed them together. "All right I'll accept that, but how could you go on all that time as if nothing was happening?"

Kiera sat down heavily on the bottom step of the stairs. "What can I say?"

"Try goodbye . . . Now piss off and leave me alone."

Kiera started to sob, first quietly and then loudly, and Grace felt awkward. Her former friend suddenly stood up and made a run for the door. "I just wanted us to be friends again . . . " she said in between howls. "You're so bloody hard, why can't you let bygones be bygones." She pushed past and staggered down the path still howling.

Grace watched her drive away and cursed to herself that she wasn't feeling any sense of satisfaction, just a humungous guilt trip.

Chapter Five

The Ringsend warehouse was kept under surveillance the following day. At about six Tony Farrell was seen entering the premises accompanied by two kids. The unit assembled discreetly outside around seven. The raid was a total fiasco, and it was obvious that the Harcourt Terrace gardaí were expected. For although the McDowells were making a video, to all intents and purposes it appeared to be a version of a very non-pornographic *Alice in Wonderland*. Philo Hoban had the title role and a spotty gurrier who looked distinctly uncomfortable, was dressed up in a caterpillar costume. They left after a token search with their tails between their legs, the derisive laughter of the McDowells and their associates ringing in their ears.

Dermot ranted and raved all the way back to Harcourt Terrace. It was fortunate that Grace was driving because he kept saying over and over, "How did they fucking know . . . how the fuck did they know?" and thumping the dashboard with his fist.

After a while Grace lost patience. "How the hell do you think they knew, Dermot . . . Flynn had it right when he said it went wrong at our end."

"What d'you mean?"

"Get real, Dermot, someone at Harcourt Terrace has to

be bent . . . it doesn't take a mastermind to figure it out."

Dermot gave the dashboard another punch, making the glove box fly open, spilling the contents over his lap, but he didn't seem to notice. "I won't have it, I don't believe it . . . If you're so sure one of us is bent, who is it? . . . Is it Jack or is it Kate or maybe it's Hugh . . . you're so smart, who's the bent fucker?"

Grace pulled into Harcourt Terrace and parked. She leaned her head on the steering wheel and closed her eyes. "I don't know who it is," she said wearily. "I don't want to start trying to think of who it could be, but after all this time, Dermot, you must realise that it's not just a case of the good guys and the bad guys, sometimes it's hard to tell the difference."

Dermot grunted, she could feel him staring at her. "You'd better come inside and ask your colleagues if they're bent or not then, hadn't you?" he said and nearly slammed the car door off its hinges.

To add insult to injury Andrew was waiting on the doorstep when she arrived home. She considered driving past but she knew that he had seen her and resigned herself to another confrontation. He smiled at her as she walked up the path unnerving her a little.

"You look tired, Grace, I suppose you're working too hard as usual."

"What do you want, Andrew?" she asked suspiciously. He shrugged still smiling and said, "Why do you assume I want something? We parted on bad terms last time . . . I just . . . "

"Stop it, Andrew . . . I don't need this," she said, fumbling for her door keys and dropping them on the step. He bent down, picked them up and opened the door for her.

"Shall we go inside?" he said. "You look as if you could use a drink." She followed him inside and slumping on the arm of the sofa gulped the large gin and tonic that he poured for her.

"Tough day?" he said.

She nodded. "Tough day."

He stood behind her and started to massage her neck and shoulders. "God, you're tense!" he said. "You should try and relax a little more, sweetheart . . . this is the stuff heart attacks are made of."

Her hackles rose to meet the tense shoulder muscles. "Well, Andrew," she said stiffly, knocking back the rest of the gin, "I suspect the fact that you ran off with my best friend, that you want to throw me out of my home, and that I'm now a social outcast may have just a tad to do with it . . . And don't call me sweetheart!" She brushed his hands away and stood up to face him. "Now . . . What do you want?"

"I see you're as unreasonable as ever," Andrew said calmly. "I don't *want* anything, Grace, I was just worried about you . . . And please don't go on about being a social outcast, I can't remember the last time we socialised together."

Grace felt foolish, it's hard to have a confrontation with someone who isn't willing to join in the spirit of the thing. "It's a bit late to start worrying about me now," she said lamely.

There was an uncomfortable silence. Andrew broke it. "Please Grace. This situation is a *fait accompli*. Can't we just be civilised . . . adult about it?"

Suddenly Grace felt very weary, she flopped down on the sofa. "OK, Andrew," she said eventually. "I'm sick and tired of fighting with you."

He patted her affectionately on the back. "You know it makes sense," he said and she nodded in reply, resigned. After a moment he said, "I was talking to your mother the other day."

"Oh yes?" she said, not really interested. She wished

41

he would leave so she could soak in a hot bath.

"Yes . . . She and my mother are throwing a lunch party for my birthday next week."

Grace's shoulders tightened up again. "So?"

Andrew shrugged. "Well, we were wondering if you'd come along? You know, just to show that there are no hard feelings."

"You're kidding. Right?"

He shook his head. "No . . . Come on, Grace, it'll be a big family party. Both families . . . yours and mine."

"And Kiera's too I suppose." Grace cast her eyes up to the ceiling. "Give me a break, Andrew. If this is what you call civilised, you can forget it."

"OK, OK," he said throwing up his hands. "I suppose it is a bit soon . . . but how about a truce?"

"Look, I'm tired, I've had a hard day. Just go will you."

He stood for a moment, not sure if they were still arguing, waiting for her to say something. When she stayed silent he said, "Well I'll be off then . . . If you change your mind, lunch is at two."

"Quit while you're ahead, Andrew," she said wearily not looking at him. He smiled to himself in the knowledge that he'd won the first battle, if not the war.

Chapter Six

Two boys playing hide-and-seek found Nicolette Power's body hanging from a tree in woodland at the edge of the Ballycoyle estate the next day. The scene bore all the appearances of a suicide until the pathologist examined the body and found the bruising round her pale thin neck inconsistent with a hanging.

"Death was due to vagal inhibition," Leo Yentob told Grace later.

"What's that?"

"In simple terms, excess pressure on the vagus nerve can cause it to send messages to the brain which orders the heart to stop . . . an instant heart attack if you like."

Where there is a suspicion of strangulation, the pathologist departs from his usual practice of opening the body from chin to pubis. Grace had attended several autopsies but she had never been at one where the victim had been strangled.

"As you see I've taken the top off the skull and removed the brain," he said.

Grace wrinkled her nose, she could feel her mouth filling with saliva and her breakfast making every effort to reappear. She swallowed hard.

"I have to leave the neck area undisturbed until I've made a further opening upwards to the breastbone, that way the blood is drained upwards and downwards from the neck area and we are left . . . " He paused and made a triumphant flourishing gesture towards the cadaver, " . . . with the coagulated blood which forms the bruising on the throat." He continued to work away, chatting as if he was doing some innocuous task.

Grace watched with horrified fascination as he sliced down the line of the sterno-mastoid muscles on either side of the neck to reveal further deep bruises on the oesophagus. "Look at the fractured thyroid cartilage and hyoid bone. And the vertebrae, no separation or trauma there. She was well dead before the murderer strung her up."

Grace had volunteered to attend the post-mortem, not because she enjoyed the duty, but because she wanted to make sure that the pathologist checked for signs of sexual abuse.

Nicolette's remains lay on the post-mortem table. The corpse was remarkably well preserved. Due to the cold weather, the process of decomposition had been significantly retarded.

"How long do you think she's been dead?" Grace asked.

Yentob thought for a moment. "Quite hard to say precisely but I would estimate about ten days at the most, five at the least, my instinct would be ten."

"So she must have died on the day she disappeared," Grace said aloud.

As he started to remove the internal organs, she stepped back and leaned against the wall. She had forgotten her menthol ointment and the smell was overpowering, though Yentob didn't seem to notice it.

"Are there any signs of sexual abuse?" she asked.

Yentob looked at her over his shoulder. "Hard to tell," he said. "There's a fair amount of bruising and swelling consistent with rape, and semen, lots of semen, so I'd say the rape was immediately before death . . . I don't know

44

if . . . Oh dear, what have we here?" he said suddenly and Grace craned her neck to see over his shoulder. "Your victim was at least two months pregnant, maybe three, poor child."

"Are you sure?" Grace said, shocked. Yentob gave her a weary look. "Sorry," she said. "Could you take foetal tissue and fluids for DNA and blood typing?"

"Of course," he said sounding irritated. And with a don't-try-and-teach-your-granddad-to-suck-eggs tone added. "What did you think I was going to do?"

Earlier Dermot had called at Leonard Power's house to inform him of his granddaughter's death which at the time had appeared to be suicide. It was a substantial and Victorian family home, hidden from any passers-by by a high well-manicured privet hedge. The doorbell jangled somewhere in the bowels of the house and it was some time before Power himself answered. Dermot explained to Power the purpose of his visit and was surprised at his apparent lack of reaction.

"I think under the circumstances it would be better if you could come down to the mortuary to identify her body, Mr Power. I understand that her mother, your daughter . . . " He let the sentence trail off.

Power looked over his shoulder and pulling the glass vestibule door closed behind him, nodded, and said in a low voice, "Yes, yes, quite so . . . " Then, "You say she killed herself . . . " His face was pallid.

"As far as we know at the moment," said Dermot.

Power stood motionless as if trying to take that in.

"The bullying I suppose, poor lamb . . . I'll come now . . . I'll just tell my wife that I'm going out."

"Aren't you going to tell her about your granddaughter?" Dermot asked, surprised.

"My wife doesn't recognise our granddaughter, Sergeant," he said, his voice still a whisper and went back

45

through the glass door, emerging a few minutes later buttoning his overcoat.

His reaction when he viewed the remains of his granddaughter was far less restrained. He wept openly. Speechless, he nodded when the sheet was pulled back from her lifeless blue-tinged face.

"So well he might weep," said Grace when Dermot described the scene later. "If you ask me he's our prime suspect, he has to be numero uno in the frame."

Dermot wasn't so sure. "I wouldn't place much store on what the Hoban girl says," he said. "But we'll see for sure when the DNA and blood type results on the body fluids come back from the lab, won't we?"

"Come on, Dermot! What about the bruising, the old man was having her left, right and centre."

"Not necessarily, we don't know it was him, it could have been the lads in the diary . . . Anto or Kevo, or someone else entirely. The murderer raped her too, remember? If Power was abusing her why didn't she mention it in the diary?"

"Maybe she was used to it, or maybe it's in last year's diary. Maybe she didn't want to admit it was happening. Philo Hoban said that Nicky didn't know that what he was doing was wrong until she put her straight . . . I'll bet he's the father of her child, the dirty bastard."

Dermot guffawed. "Didn't know it was wrong? . . . Come on, give me a break, if he was interfering with her she must have known it was wrong. And before you say it I know that doesn't mean she necessarily liked it but I still think there would have been some reference to it in the diary."

"Well he has to be questioned," she said stubbornly. Dermot's attitude was making her ratty.

"Of course, but so has the mother, the neighbours, Anto and Kevo whoever, her teachers, classmates," he was counting off on his fingers. "So we'd better get down to

Harcourt Square before O'Keefe blows his top, hadn't we?"

The phone rang just then and Grace picked it up. "de Rossa," she said.

"Is that Grace?" a small voice asked.

Grace recognised it as belonging to Philo. "Yes . . . is that you, Philo?"

"Is Nicky dead? It said on the telly she's dead."

"Yes, Philo, she was murdered . . . listen could we talk, you could be able to help." Philo didn't answer and Grace could feel her reticence over the phone line.

"Please, anything you tell me will be in confidence, I promise."

"You won't drag me into court or back to the friggin' children's home?" Grace reaffirmed her promise.

"OK. I'll meet you in twenty minutes at the café on the corner of Lower Liffey Street, but I don't think I know anythin' that'll help." With that she hung up abruptly.

"Tell the boss I've gone to meet the Hoban girl, will you?" Grace said to Dermot as she grabbed her coat and bag. "I don't want to chance being late in case she doesn't wait."

Grace didn't see Philo at first when she entered the café. She was sitting in the far corner away from the steamy windows. Grace bought two cups of coffee and a couple of chocolate biscuits and made her way over. Philo was smoking, her fingers were nicotine stained, the nails bitten down to the quick. Without even a greeting she launched into, "What happened, it said on the telly she was hung?"

"She was raped as well, Philo. It's dangerous on the streets, you should know that."

"She wasn't on the streets, no one saw her on the streets. I'd have bumped into her . . . I'd have looked out for her, poor cow." She was getting upset.

47

Grace patted her hand. " OK. If you say so . . . Did you know that she kept a diary?" The girl shook her head. Grace continued, "She mentioned Anto and Kevo in it, d'you know who they are?"

"Anto works in Video Paradise . . . I think he might own it, Anto Farrell's his name . . . You saw him where we were makin' the film the other night . . . "

"You mean Tony Farrell?" Grace said surprised.

"Yeh . . . Anto . . . Tony . . . whatever, I know him as Anto."

"What about the other one, Kevo?"

"He's just a spotty gurrier that hangs round there. You saw him too, he was the eejit dressed up as the fuckin' insect when we was makin' the film, though I still say it's the auld fella you should be talkin' to."

Grace didn't mention that she had the same suspicion, instead she said, "Why d'you say that?"

Philo sighed. "I told you, he was messin' with her."

"When was the last time you saw her?"

Philo thought for a moment. "I think it musta been the day before she went missin'. We went to the Paradise after she came outa school . . . she was hooked on sonic hedgehogs. She didn't stay that long, she said her ma was sick again."

"Was Anto there, can you remember?"

"Yeh," she said nodding. "He was always there, he came over and let us have a couple of free gos. He liked Nicky, he used to tell her jokes to make her laugh."

"And did she leave before you?"

Philo nodded. "Yeh . . . I'd no home to go to remember!" she said and smiled. "And don't forget you promised you'd not send me back to the welfare." After the fiasco of the video shoot Philo had been taken by a social worker into care, though everyone involved knew that they were only going through the motions and that she would abscond as soon as she got the chance.

48

"You'd be better off if you went back home to your mother, you know," Grace said, knowing very well it was a waste of energy to take her back to the children's home again. "Tony Farrell's no good, he'll have you making blue films or worse if you're not careful, and we had word that his bosses are sending kids out of the country . . . did you hear anything about that?"

"No . . . I didn't hear nothing about that," Philo said irritably. "But I don't do nothin' I don't want to . . . can I go now?"

"Whenever you want," Grace said. "But be careful. It's dangerous on the street, no matter how streetwise you think you are. Apart from anything else you could catch a very nasty disease." She got no response from Philo who just stared blankly at her. After a minute Grace added, "Anyway thanks for ringing me. If you hear anything will you call me again? And please be careful."

"OK." Philo answered getting to her feet and casting her eyes to the ceiling. "I'll be careful, I know about safe sex you know . . . I'm not stupid." She paused at the corner of the table and Grace thought at that instant that she looked about thirty years old.

"Poor Nicky wasn't safer at home, was she?"

Grace felt that under the circumstances she couldn't argue with that sentiment so she didn't answer and just watched as the girl gave her a nod and walked out of the café back into Liffey Street.

49

Chapter Seven

Grace called at Leonard Power's home on her way back to Harcourt Terrace. The Power residence was situated at the better end of Sandymount village. A plump middle-aged woman, whom she later discovered was the housekeeper, answered the bell after an interval and left Grace standing in the dark wood-panelled hall while she disappeared to announce her arrival to Power. The feel and smell of her surroundings reminded Grace of a convent. Pictures of stern saints, eyes cast heavenward, cluttered the walls and the smell of beeswax polish assaulted her nostrils. The squeak of crêpe-soled shoes on the over-polished lino announced the housekeeper's return. "This way," she said, opening the door to one of the front reception rooms. The drawing-room had the same unlived in air as the hall, and although the sun streamed through the window, it didn't add any feeling of welcome.

Leonard Power was shocked and outraged when Grace interviewed him and mentioned as delicately as she could Philo Hoban's assertion that he had abused his granddaughter and the fact that she was nearly three months pregnant. Hatchett hadn't wanted her to confront him at all, being of the same mind as Dermot, that if Philo was right, why wasn't there any mention of abuse in Nicky's (now missing) diary.

He claimed that the last occasion that he had seen Nicky was the nineteenth, two days before she disappeared, and when Grace tackled him about his movements on the day Nicky was last seen, he said that he had been home for two days suffering from an attack of flu and that was the reason he had not seen either Nicky or his daughter between the nineteenth and the morning Ann had reported Nicky missing. Ann Power had told the same story when Dermot interviewed her, and it was she who claimed to have lost Nicky's diary when he asked to see it again. She also said that Nicky had only started to keep a diary at the beginning of the year.

"Would there be anyone who could corroborate your alibi, Mr Power?" Grace asked. She thought he was going to have a heart attack. "How dare you, young woman! . . . how dare you doubt what I am saying," he fumed, his face turning puce. "Do you seriously think that I would harm a hair of her head? What you suggest is grotesque and obscene."

"I'm sorry, Mr Power, but the fact is, rape and murder *are* grotesque and obscene and the only way we can find the person responsible is by a process of elimination, so if you would cooperate it would make our job a lot easier." Grace's placid reaction to his outburst disarmed him and he looked embarrassed. Although her tone was friendly, really she was thinking, *come on you filthy pervert . . . admit it . . . admit that you've been raping your granddaughter, that you made her pregnant and then you throttled the life out of her.* She just smiled at him though and said, "Perhaps Mrs Power could help."

"Perhaps," he said crisply. "Though as I told you, Assumpta doesn't know that I supported my granddaughter or that I see Ann, so I would rather you didn't mention why you want to know about my movements."

51

Grace was amazed. "You mean you still haven't told her about Nicky?"

Power looked down at the carpet. "No, I don't want to upset her," he said avoiding eye contact.

"Upset her! . . . Mr Power, she has a right to know that her granddaughter is dead."

"You're not listening to me, Garda de Rossa. In my wife's eyes she has no granddaughter . . . I don't want her to know that I've been seeing her . . . do you understand?"

"I understand what you're saying, Mr Power, and if that's what you want I don't have to mention why I need to know, but don't you think she may be just a bit curious. And anyway surely she's seen the papers and the RTE news, she must know that Nicky's dead."

"You're still not listening to me . . . Assumpta doesn't know who Nicky is."

"I see . . . Could I speak to your wife?"

Power hesitated. "What are you going to say . . . what reason are you going to give her for your enquiry?"

"I'll say it's to do with a traffic incident."

He thought about that, then nodded. "Very well, please come this way." He led Grace into the hall and up the sturdy mahogany staircase to a front bedroom. Assumpta Power sat in a wheelchair by the window, a rosary beads clasped loosely in her hands. She turned towards the door when her husband and Grace entered. Her features were gaunt, but Grace supposed that in her heyday Assumpta Power would have been a good-looking woman, and in better health she would still have been handsome.

"This is Detective Garda de Rossa, my dear," he said. "She would like to ask you a few questions."

"What about?" she snapped.

Grace stepped forward. "A motorist made a complaint that a car sideswiped his van and he gave Mr Power's licence number. We need to know where your husband was on the nineteenth and twentieth and twenty-first of March."

"Doesn't the person know which day his van was hit?" Assumpta said sarcastically.

"No, he can't remember which day it was." She thought it sounded just about as plausible as Assumpta not knowing about her granddaughter.

"Hmmph . . . how is he so sure about the licence number then?"

Grace was ready for this. "He wasn't sure . . . he gave us three versions of the number and we're checking them all out," she said.

The explanation seemed to satisfy Assumpta and she said after a minute or two's thought, "Leonard was ill in bed on those days . . . I particularly remember because he was unable to help me downstairs and I had to stay up here all day. So you see, he could not possibly have been involved."

"Thank you, Mrs Power," Grace said and turned to leave. When she got to the door she stopped. "One more thing . . . were you in each other's company all that time?"

Leonard Power's face turned to fury. "For heaven's sake, Garda de Rossa, of course not. I was sleeping most of the time . . . I was ill for God's sake!"

Grace smiled up at him. "Thank you, Mr Power, you've been very helpful."

Once again this had the effect of diffusing the situation and with a supreme effort to keep his voice calm and even, for the benefit of his spouse he said, "Very well . . . I'll see you out." He looked over at where his wife was sitting in her wheelchair, once again mouthing silent Hail Marys.

"Goodbye, Mrs Power," Grace called over her shoulder but Assumpta didn't look up.

Power led her down to the front door. "I shall be making a complaint to your superiors, de Rossa," he said as she walked towards her car. "Your handling of this unfortunate situation has been insensitive to say the very least."

"That's your prerogative, Mr Power," she said. "But I would have thought you would be only too anxious to assist us in this enquiry, after all your granddaughter has been brutally raped and murdered."

Power's face froze and she could feel his glare as she drove out into Park Avenue. She looked back at the house and, just visible above the high hedge, she could see Assumpta Power watching her through the upstairs window.

When she pulled up in front of Harcourt Terrace she saw Dermot on his way out. He walked over to the car and got in. "O'Keefe wants us to talk to Tony Farrell," he said. "How did you get on with Power?"

"The wife confirmed his alibi, but I don't know . . . he could easily have left the house without her knowledge, she's in a wheelchair."

Dermot grunted. "My money's on Farrell."

"Why Farrell for God's sake?" she said, though she wasn't really surprised at his statement. "You're just looking for a reason to link it to the McDowells . . . I think you're way off base Dermot."

"We'll see," he said and left it at that.

Grace parked in Cathal Brugha Street and they fought their way across O'Connell Street and down Henry Street through the tide of rush hour pedestrians and late shoppers. It was dusk and the lights from the shop windows spilled out into the street. Moore Street, where they were heading, is just off Henry Street which is one of the busiest shopping streets in Europe. Moore Street is famous for the women stall-holders who sell the best fruit, veg, flowers and fish in the city. They waded through the small mountains of waste packing and apple cartons as the women started to pack away their stalls for the night.

"Ligh'ers . . . two fer a pow-end!" yelled a thin youth.

"Ballooo-ens . . . fifty peeee!" yelled another.

"Well hello, Mister McEvoy . . . Would yez like a bag of apples to take home wit yez?" called one of the women.

"Why don't yez just take Fidelma?" shouted another roaring with laughter. "She'd keep yez warm at nigh'!"

Dermot grinned and collected the bag of fruit. "Thanks, Fidelma, no offence but I'll just take the apples." He bit into one and tossed another over to Grace.

Video Paradise was half way down the street in a basement. A downward pointing neon arrow flashing on and off indicated the doorway which led down a narrow flight of stairs. The accidental visitor could be left in no doubt as to what lay in the dimly lit subterranean space. Electronic buzzing, beeping and burbling noises emanated upwards.

They made their way towards a kiosk in the corner where more neon bulbs flashed the message *Change.*

Into what? thought Grace looking round at the customers, zombie-like at their machines, punching buttons and joy-sticks in hypnotic concentration. Occasionally one of them would give a whoop and thump the side of the machine or let off a string of curses and pour more money into an ever-hungry slot.

"Is Tony Farrell about?" Dermot asked, holding his warrant card up to the glass. A young girl of about seventeen with curly blonde hair, black roots and bad skin stopped in mid-chew and peered at the card. She slid off her high stool and said, "I'll go see," before vanishing through a door at the rear of the booth.

Grace looked round the room. It was surprisingly long and obviously lay beneath several of the overhead buildings. A security camera suspended from the ceiling was pointing in the direction of the entrance and another towards the far corner at the change kiosk. She nudged Dermot and drew his attention to them.

A few minutes later the girl returned. "You're to go in," she said, pointing at a door beside the kiosk as she climbed back onto her perch.

The office beyond the door was blissfully silent after the white noise outside and it was only after the door closed behind her that Grace realised that the noise had caused her neck and shoulder muscles to tighten, so she relaxed.

Tony aka Anto Farrell was sitting behind a battered desk, his chair tilted on the two back legs. He was an unattractive young man of about twenty, with acned skin and short stubby hair. On his temples he wore the customary blue dot tattoo that all graduates of Dublin's famous penal institution, Mountjoy Prison, wear with pride.

"Mr McEvoy," he said. "What can I do for yeh?"

"We're investigating the murder of Nicolette Power," Dermot said curtly. "We have reason to believe she used to come here to play the machines with a girl called Philo Hoban." He placed the victim's photograph on the desk in front of Tony Farrell.

He looked down at it briefly, then shrugged and said, "Maybe," non-commitally, "she looks familiar . . . I don't remember the last time she was in."

"We know for sure that she was here the day before she disappeared, on the twentieth, with the Hoban girl, do you know if she came in the day after on her own?"

Farrell shook his head again. "Maybe, I wouldn't know for sure." Grace looked round the room. It was cluttered and dusty. A large cardboard carton of video cassettes caught her eye and she peered into the box to see if she could read the labels. Farrell noticed what she was doing and started to laugh. "Them are security videos, missus, don't bother lookin' for iffy cassettes here."

Grace gave him a sweet smile. "Actually it was security videos that I was looking for, Tony." She flipped through the tapes reading the dates on the labels and picked out four. "She'd be on these if she was in, wouldn't she?"

Farrell frowned. "Yeh I suppose so . . . though I don't remember seein' her."

"You do remember the girl though, don't you?" Dermot said sarcastically. "She was a friend of your potential film starlet after all."

"Wha'? . . . Well yeh . . . I remember her . . . thin kid," he said. "She usually came in with Philo Hoban, I don't remember her coming in on her own at all."

"Well this should tell us one way or another," Grace said holding up the cassettes. "We'll let you have them back as soon as we've finished with them."

Farrell looked alarmed. "I don't think yeh can take them tapes," he said, reaching out a hand to grab them from Grace. "Have yeh got a warrant?"

Grace laughed. "Now why would we need one of those Tony? Surely you want to help us catch the killer . . . anyway you know we can get one inside the hour."

Farrell hesitated, then let go. "I suppose it's OK then," he said dubiously.

"Fucking right it's OK, Farrell," said Dermot. "You wouldn't want me to do you for obstructing justice, would you?"

"Where were you on the twentieth and twenty-first from say . . . three onwards?" Grace asked.

"I dunno . . . If I'd known I'd need an alibi I'd've kept a fuckin' diary. But I suppose I was here till after nine when we closed for the night, I always am."

"So who was minding the store at seven the other

57

night when you were contributing to Irish cultural life?" Grace asked.

"Wha'?" Farrell said, looking perplexed.

"Who was here while you were making the film in Ringsend, moron?"

"It was my night off, Carina was here, but look . . . I didn't kill the kid . . . I never saw her except in here." He was beginning to sound anxious and his arrogance was evaporating fast.

"Well we'll see about that, Tony," Grace said. "But don't be so uptight . . . If you're innocent you know you've nothing to worry about."

Farrell gave a snorting laugh. "Bollix!" he said. "I've heard that one before."

As they were turning to leave Dermot said, "Don't forget, Farrell, I'm watching you, I'll have you and the McDowells if it's the last thing I do."

Farrell, who was sitting on the edge of his desk tried to muster some bravado and shouted after them, "Count on it, Mr McEvoy . . . yeh won't live that long."

The incident room was being run for convenience by the Serious Crime Squad at the Central Detective Unit in Harcourt Square just down the street from Harcourt Terrace Garda Station and it was a hive of activity when they returned and handed in their reports. The house-to-house team had come up with several possible sightings of Nicky, all which had to be followed up, and the phones were hot after both the *Evening Herald* and *Press* had published Nicky's picture with a request for information.

They hung around for a further half hour to watch the security videos, then signed off duty and went to the pub. Jack Mulloy had arrived just ahead of them and was propping up the bar when they walked into Smyths, deep in conversation with Jimmy the barman.

He ordered a round and went over to join them at a table. "What d'you think?" he said. They both knew what he was talking about.

"My money's on the grandfather, Dermot fancies Tony Farrell or the McDowells."

"I'll give you five to one on the grandfather, odds on on Farrell and evens on the McDowells," Jack said, taking out a notebook and biro.

"I'll take a tenner's worth on Power at five to one," Grace said handing him over two fivers. Jack took the money from her hand and wrote in his note book.

"Sucker!" she said grinning.

"You're the sucker . . . didn't you see the security video?" Jack said.

"I saw it, I just don't think he did it that's all."

"She's got a bee in her bonnet about Power," Dermot said to Jack. "Never mind the fact that Farrell lied about the girl being there the day she disappeared."

"I know she was on the tape," Grace snapped. "But Farrell wasn't there at the same time as the girl, so how do we know he saw her?"

"Because he said he was there till nine both nights."

"Maybe . . . but they're not on the tape together are they . . . it's possible that he didn't even know she was in . . . "

Both men guffawed. "OK smart arse," she said, looking straight at Dermot. "Don't you think he'd have wiped the only evidence against him if he had killed her?"

Dermot stopped laughing and adopted the sort of tone that an adult would use when trying to explain a simple task to a stupid child. "Not necessarily, Grace, it might not have crossed his fucking evil little mind, he's not that smart . . . say goodbye to your tenner, by this time tomorrow he'll be charged, and with a bit of luck, if he's the little shit I think he is, he'll probably have dragged the McDowells down with him. Mark my words . . . he's in the frame for this one, and if he is, so are they."

"Now who has the bee in the bonnet?" Grace said irritably and the two men looked at each other and cast their eyes heavenwards.

They sat in silence round the table, staring into their drinks. The exchange had left Grace in bad humour and after a while she drained her glass and got to her feet. "Well I'm off," she said. "All this heavy deduction is far too much for a mere woman to cope with."

They watched as she stalked down the bar to the back door. "What's the matter with her?" Jack said.

"Who knows," said Dermot. "Must be that PTM or whatever they call it." The two men nodded and went back to their drinks.

Chapter Eight

Tony Farrell was brought to Harcourt Square early the following morning for questioning. He refused to say a word until Pongo Strong, his solicitor, had arrived, then he denied all knowledge of seeing Nicky Power on the day of her disappearance.

Superintendent Con O'Keefe and Dermot were sitting in the interview room across the table from the two men.

Farrell was lounging in his seat apparently unconcerned with a smug smirk on his face, but his body language gave away his hidden anxiety as the smoke from the cigarette in his shaking hand zig-zagged into the air towards the ceiling.

"So you still claim that Nicky Power didn't visit Video Paradise on the twenty-first?"

Farrell, avoiding eye contact, snapped, "How many times do I have to tell yeh . . . I never saw her . . . the video proves it."

O'Keefe nodded to Dermot. "We have two witnesses who claim to have seen you at the Ringsend warehouse at six-fifteen on the evening of the twenty-first with a girl answering Nicky's description."

Farrell shot a look at Strong who said quickly, before his client could speak, "Are the witnesses certain that it was my client that they actually saw?"

Dermot smiled and looking straight at Farrell said, "Absolutely certain, they know him well."

"They're lyin', I was never at the warehouse with the Power girl."

"Forensic may disagree with you when we get blood type and DNA back . . . What's your blood group, Tony?"

He started to speak, then changed his mind about the content and said, "I want to speak to Mr Strong alone."

O'Keefe and Dermot left the room and stood in the corridor.

"I think that'll have him on the run," Dermot said.

O'Keefe was more subdued. "Perhaps, we need blood samples from him though. If he's an 'A' secretor that puts us one step nearer and makes it a one-in-ten chance it's him until the DNA result comes back."

"I'd put money on that he is."

The door opened and Strong came out. "My client would like to make a statement, but he's in a difficult position with regard to his employers."

"Such as?" said O'Keefe.

"Come on, Superintendent, you know who he works for, you know if he falls foul of them it could seriously damage his health."

"Are you saying that the McDowells are involved in Nicolette Power's murder?" Dermot said, feeling a rush of hope.

"No. I'm not," said Strong emphatically. "I'm saying that my client's alibi may embarrass him with regard to his employers, so, as you can understand, he's rather reluctant for obvious reasons."

"That's his problem," said Dermot. "If he's no alibi then he's in the frame for Nicky Power's murder, and if his alibi puts the McDowells away, I for one won't weep any tears."

"What's the embarrassment?" O'Keefe said.

"My client hasn't confided in me on that point as yet.

But he's willing to talk to you if he can avoid any prosecution that may follow the disclosure."

"Come on, Strong, you know it doesn't work like that . . . he can go down for a murder he says he didn't commit or he can get into bother with the McDowells and us, it's up to you to advise him which is the lesser of the two evils."

Strong stood looking at the wall thinking through what O'Keefe had just said. After a moment or two he said, "I'll speak to my client again," and went back through the door. Dermot leaned against the wall and O'Keefe stood with his hands in his pockets waiting to see how Strong would advise Farrell. Five minutes later the door opened and Strong poked his head out. "Mr Farrell would like to make a statement," he said.

A blue haze of smoke hung in the air when they re-entered the room. Farrell was smoking yet another cigarette, holding it between his index finger and thumb, cupped into the palm of his hand.

"OK, Farrell, what have you got to tell us?" O'Keefe said sitting on the corner of the table.

"I met Nicky outside the club at about a quarter past six."

"Accidentally?"

Farrell shook his head. "No, I'd arranged to meet her, though I didn't know she'd been inside the club earlier." He slumped his head down into his shoulders and lapsed into silence.

"Why had you arranged to meet?"

Farrell mumbled something.

"What?" said Dermot.

"I was givin' her money."

"What for?!"

"She was doin' photos for me, I was payin' her for the ones she done already."

"What kind of photos?"

63

Farrell shifted in his seat. "Glamour shots, yeh know?"

"You can't mean page three shots, she was only a child. Were they heavier altogether?" O'Keefe said.

Farrell shrugged. "There wasn't any harm . . . and I didn't lay a finger on her, I swear."

"OK," said Dermot. "What happened then, where do the McDowells come in?"

Farrell was sweating. He wiped his brow with the back of his hand. "I was usin' their equipment and sellin' the pictures on . . . they don't know about it . . . they'd kill me if they found out I was usin' their stuff and not givin' them a cut . . . I dropped her at the bus stop at about seven and went on to Branden's Snooker Club in Fenian Street. She was fine when I left her, Mr O'Keefe . . . on my mother's life."

"Your mother's dead, Farrell," said Dermot flatly. "Did you have sex with her?"

Tony Farrell shook his head violently back and forth. "No way, Mr McEvoy . . . No way . . . she was just a kid."

"But old enough to take filthy pictures of?" Dermot shouted, his face inches from Farrell's.

"Go on with the story," O'Keefe said. "Why did you have to take her to Ringsend to pay her the money, why didn't you just give it to her outside the club?"

"I wanted to have a talk with her, I liked the kid . . . I wanted to put some more work her way, that's all."

"What kind of work?" asked O'Keefe.

Farrell just shrugged. "Yeh know . . . " He didn't elaborate further and all three men stood looking down at him in silence waiting for him to go on.

The silence lengthened and Dermot prompted, "No, Tony, we don't know, we're waiting for you to tell us."

He looked up at them. "She told me she needed money and that she wanted to leave home like Philo Hoban . . . she wanted to do what the Hoban girl's doin'."

"Which is . . . " said O'Keefe in exasperation.

"She wanted to go on the game, she wanted me to help her get started."

Dermot gave a derisory laugh. "You're trying to say that Nicky Power asked you to help her to go on the game?"

"On my life, Mr McEvoy," he said with his hand on his heart. "May God strike me dead if I'm lyin'."

Dermot looked at O'Keefe who shrugged and raised his eyebrows. "I don't believe you, Farrell . . . Nicky Power lived a sheltered life for the past fourteen years with no friends bar her mother and grandfather, she was a child for God's sake, and you're trying to tell us she wanted to become a prostitute."

"She was no child . . . far from it!" Farrell burst out. "She had the come-hither that one, she was no little virgin. She said she might as well get paid for it as not."

"What did she mean?"

"Philo Hoban said that the auld fella was havin' her left, right an' centre, work it out for yerself."

O'Keefe inclined his head towards the door and Dermot followed his back out into the corridor. "What d'you think?" he said.

"I think he's grasping at straws."

"Yes, but what about Leonard Power?"

Dermot shook his head. "I don't know, the only source of that allegation so far is the Hoban girl, I still think Nicky would have mentioned it in her diary if he'd been abusing her, especially since she got to know Philo Hoban and she put her straight as she claimed."

"Don't forget she was over two months pregnant, that would probably pre-date her friendship with Tony Farrell."

"Only as far as we know, but then I think there's a lot we don't know about Nicolette Power."

"You know Power hit the roof and complained to the

65

Commissioner when de Rossa mentioned the abuse allegation to him."

"That's a bit over the top, isn't it?"

"I think they're both members of the same golf club or something like that."

"Suppose we talk to Ann Power about it, start by asking her about the pregnancy . . . see how she reacts?"

O'Keefe nodded. "Yes, go over with de Rossa after we've finished here. Get her to do the talking. I think Ann Power will open up to Grace better than to you. Now let's see what else the brave Tony has to say for himself." They re-entered the room and O'Keefe sat back on the edge of the table and Dermot leaned against the wall.

"Go on with your story, Tony."

"Where was I up to?" he said looking at Strong.

"You dropped her off at the bus stop at seven . . . " Strong said.

"Oh yeh . . . After I dropped her I went on to Branden's as I said. And Alan, me and a few others stayed till after midnight."

"Is that it?" asked Dermot with surprise. "That's your alibi?"

"Yeh won't tell Branden that I was sellin' the pictures, will ye?" said Farrell, more concerned with Branden McDowell then with the fact that his alibi was feeble to say the least.

"Tony, your alibi stinks. You could easily have raped and strangled her before you went to the club, then gone back later to dump the body in Ballycoyle woods . . . I thought you were going to come up with something decent," said Dermot. "Forensic can prove if you raped her you know."

"I told yeh I didn't rape her . . . she wanted it."

"What are you saying?" said O'Keefe. "Are you admitting that you had sex with the girl?"

"It wasn't like that . . . she wanted it. I was fond of her . . . I wouldn't hurt her."

"Sure!" said Dermot. "And I suppose you didn't strangle the life out of her either . . . You wouldn't hurt her but you'd pimp for her and have underage sex . . . That's statutory rape you know?"

Farrell was getting distressed, he put his head in his hands and mumbled, "I told yeh . . . I didn' rape her."

"If she's underage it counts as rape, Tony, you know that," O'Keefe said. "How long had you been having relations with Nicolette Power, Tony?"

He looked up and shrugged. "Couple of months . . . I can't remember . . . but I didn' rape her . . . whatever ye say."

"Did you know she was pregnant?"

Farrell's expression said that he definitely did not know that. He didn't speak and just shook his head. "Oh Jeasus!" he muttered.

"OK. When did you first meet her?"

Looking down at his shoes, Farrell thought for a moment. "January I think . . . yes it was definitely January."

"And when did you first have sex with her?"

"I don't remember . . . but the kid wasn't mine. Someone else raped her after I left her at the bus stop . . . I didn't kill her . . . "

"We'll see about that," said O' Keefe. "Where's your car?"

"Why?"

"Forensic will want to go over it."

Farrell took the keys from his pocket. "It's outside the club," he said. "But you won't find nothin' in it. I didn't kill her."

"Then you've nothing to worry about," said O'Keefe. "I think that's enough for the moment, we'll talk again tomorrow."

Farrell stood up. "Can I go now?" he said looking relieved.

"No, we want you where we can find you and the police surgeon will take a blood sample if you've no objection." Farrell shrugged. "Anyway you'll be safer here in case your friend Branden finds out about your little business venture."

Strong started to make an objection but Farrell obviously thought O'Keefe's reasoning was sound. "That's OK, Mr Strong. I'll stay here," he said.

There was no answer to Ann Power's door bell and the curtains were drawn. "She can't be out . . . she never goes out," said Grace. "D'you think she's OK?"

Dermot pushed the bell again. "The house sounds empty," he said. "I'll go and look through the back. See if the neighbours have seen her."

Grace walked next door and before she could ring the bell the door was opened by a well-built woman in her sixties. "You lookin' for her next door?" she asked, indicating Ann Power's house with her head.

"Yes, d'you know if she's in, she isn't answering the bell?"

The woman scratched her head. "Queer," she said peering over the hedge. "I never heard her go out . . . It was her young wan got done in y'know?"

"Yes, I know," said Grace. "Do you know her well?"

The woman shook her head. "Kept herself to herself . . . the kid was a bright wan though." She looked down at the ground. "Sad . . . very sad. God rest her, and curse the one that kilt her."

"You say you didn't hear her going out?"

The woman nodded. "S'right . . . she must be lyin' down poor thing, she mighta taken a tablet or somethin'."

A thought struck Grace. "Thanks," she said to the

68

woman and ran back to Ann Power's side of the hedge. "Dermot!" she called urgently, trying the front door. He hurried round the side of the building.

"What's up?"

"I think she may have taken tablets or something, the woman next door says she's in."

"Yeh, that's right," called the woman who was on the other side of the hedge watching them. Dermot put his elbow through the small pane of glass in the front door and reached in to open the Yale. The house was deathly quiet. Grace ran upstairs and Dermot went into the darkened living-room.

Ann Power was lying on her bed unconscious, two empty tablet bottles beside her on the bed.

"She's up here," shouted Grace feeling for a pulse. It was weak but there. She started shaking the inert body. "Come on, Ann . . . wake up," she said, but the woman didn't stir. "Radio for an ambulance!" she called as Dermot reached the top of the stairs. "She's taken an overdose."

Ann was very near to death by the time the ambulance got her to St James's Hospital. Grace stayed there until late in the hope that she would regain consciousness. At about nine o'clock Leonard Power hurried in.

"How is she, how is my daughter?"

"Very poorly, Mr Power," Grace said coldly. "She took an overdose, the doctors said another twenty minutes and she wouldn't have survived."

His face was ashen. "All this awful business has been too much for her. My poor, poor poppet."

"I found her," Grace said.

Power looked at her enduringly. "How? . . . what were you doing at her house?"

"I was going to ask her a few questions about Nicky."

His mouth started to twitch and his eyes narrowed.

"What questions?" he said.

Grace shrugged. "Routine questions. You know . . . everyday things like *do you know your daughter was two months pregnant? And what about your father, was he sexually abusing her,* those sort of things."

Power's face went puce and he grabbed hold of her lapel. "Enough!" he said. "How dare you say those filthy things, you slut." Grace took hold of his hand and tried to wrestle it from her coat, but she couldn't loosen his grip. His face was only inches from hers and she could feel his damp breath on her face. "You'll be finished when I've done with you, lady," he hissed. Suddenly he dropped her lapel and clutched at his head. Grace stepped back and he gave a strangled gasp before crumpling to the floor in a convulsion. She was stunned and stood where she was for an instant before realisation dawned on her, Christ! I've made the bastard have a stroke, she thought and rushed up the corridor to call a nurse.

"What happened?" Dermot asked when he returned to hospital later on.

"He just had a stroke," she said.

"Just like that?"

"Just like that," she said innocently.

Chapter Nine

Grace wasn't due on duty until two the following afternoon but she got up at six with the intention of going in early anyway. She wondered how Ann and Leonard Power were, and if Assumpta Power was yet aware that her daughter and husband were on the brink of death, and that her husband had probably raped and murdered her granddaughter. She was musing on these thoughts when there was a pounding on the front door. She hurried out to open it, and as she did four burly men pushed their way in. "Detective Inspector Killery, Garda Complaints," said the leader of the group, holding up a warrant card.

He thrust a sheet of typed paper into her hand. "This is a copy of the complaint we've received against you which we're investigating."

Grace was stunned. "What are you talking about? What's this all about?" As she was saying this, two of them ran up the stairs and the third hurried through to the kitchen. "Where are going . . . You can't do this . . . "

She started up the stairs after the two officers but Killery grabbed her arm. "Just read the complaint, de Rossa. I have to warn you that anything you say at this time may be . . . "

"Why are you cautioning me . . . what am I supposed to have done?" She was becoming frantic.

Killery forced the paper up to her face. "Just read the complaint, de Rossa."

She looked at the sheet of paper but her eyes wouldn't take in the words. Killery said, "You've the right to have a solicitor present or your GRA rep . . . I think it'd be a good idea."

Grace was still open-mouthed, suddenly she pulled herself together. "Look . . . this is stupid, you can't do this, who made this complaint . . . "

"Up here sir," shouted one of the two men on the floor above and Killery pushed past her up the stairs. She ran after him into her bedroom.

"What is it, Declan?" he said to the officer standing by her open wardrobe, then she saw he was holding a plastic cash card gingerly by the edge.

"What's that?" she asked.

"You tell me," Killery said as he took it carefully from Declan and read the name pressed into the plastic. "Who's Michael King?"

"How would I know . . . I've never seen that card before." Now she was really panicking. "It's nothing to do with me."

"If you take the trouble to read the complaint, de Rossa, you'll see that you're accused of receiving corrupt payments from a building society account in the name of Michael King."

"Bullshit. Who from?"

Killery took out an evidence bag and dropped the plastic card inside. "We've reason to believe that the payments are from Branden McDowell . . . "

Killery continued to speak but she couldn't take in what he was saying, the blood was pounding in her head and she thought she was going to faint. Killery was still rabbiting on and Declan and the other goon were emptying her underwear out of the drawers of her dressing-table. The whole situation was surreal. Suddenly she was furious. *"Stop!"* she shouted with such volume that the three men froze. "Stop," she said again in a more normal voice. "I know you're just doing your job, but that doesn't give you the right to violate my house . . . I've been set up . . . can't you see that . . . "

Killery gave her a weary look. "Of course you have, de Rossa, of course you have . . . now can we get on with it . . . Please." They went on pulling the room apart and from downstairs she heard the sound of crashing crockery followed by a muffled curse. Grace turned and ran down to the kitchen. The officer was crouching on the floor picking up the shards of a broken jug, he looked up apologetically. "Sorry," he said and went back to what he was doing.

This is a nightmare she said to herself running to the phone. Hands shaking she dialled Kiera's number. It rang and rang. "Come on . . . " she said urgently into the receiver, and after what seemed like an age, Andrew answered. He sounded half asleep and it took a few minutes for him to unscramble her incoherent babble.

"I'll be right over," he said crisply and hung up.

Killery walked downstairs as she was replacing the receiver. "I have to take your warrant card, de Rossa, you'll be suspended from duty as of now, and I need your bank statements . . . where d'you keep them?"

"I want you to wait until my solicitor gets here. I want to take advice."

Killery shrugged. "Suit yourself," he said wandering through to the kitchen and sitting at the table.

Grace followed. "You haven't told me who made this complaint."

He looked up at her and said. "I thought you wanted to wait for your solicitor."

It was Grace's turn to say "Suit yourself."

An hour and a half later Grace sat at the same table with Andrew. The interlopers had gone and she was still in a state of shock. She told him about the two disastrous operations involving the McDowells and of her suspicion that one of the unit must be on their pay-roll.

Andrew read through the complaint again. "I've never dealt with one of these before," he said. "But as far as I know the onus is on them to prove your guilt as opposed to you having to prove yourself innocent."

"That's not much consolation . . . So what happens now?"

Andrew put the sheet of paper down on the table-top. "There didn't appear to be any moneys that you couldn't account for on the bank statements?" There was a question mark at the end of the sentence.

"What d'you mean didn't appear to be . . . there wasn't . . . isn't. Whose side are you on?"

"Calm down, woman. I'm just trying to assess what they have against you." He moved over to the kitchen sink where he stood with his back to her. After a while he turned and said, "Right . . . All they seem to have is the complaint and the card which they can't prove you used." She opened her mouth to speak but he held up his hand to silence her. "I've demanded that they check the card for prints, yours can't be on it if you've never seen it before. Then there's the fact that the card is in a man's name. If the account was set up for you, it would be more sensible to open the account in a woman's name."

"You don't sound very convinced," she said sourly.

"For Christ's sake, Grace, drop the paranoia will you. We've yet to see the building society statements. Presumably the idea of the card is for simplicity . . . "

"What d'you mean?"

"With the card you can withdraw money without incriminating yourself. You don't have to ever go near the branch where the account is on deposit, you just need a PIN number . . . clever isn't it?"

Despite being seriously worried by her predicament, Grace had to admit she was impressed. "Yes . . . But what about deposits?"

"Same idea. The money can be deposited in cash anywhere, probably by a different person each time."

"Can the building society check the actual times of the cash point withdrawals?"

"Good thinking," said Andrew. "Both the location and the time should be on record, so that's a starting point. Hopefully whoever it is that has set you up isn't on the same duties as you, and the money was withdrawn at the other end of the country, preferably while you were in court!"

"What really bothers me is why whoever it is that's taking the shilling would risk the wrath of the McDowells."

Andrew snorted. "What risk? What wrath? The whole point of the exercise is to take the heat off themselves. There's no proof that the money's coming from the McDowells, only an allegation. So by pointing the finger at you they can achieve that end and after a short interval they can all be back in business." There was a brief silence then Andrew said, "Who do you think it is?"

"I haven't a clue, it's hard to imagine any one of the unit being bent . . . I mean I know some of them cut corners from time to time, but that's in the name of getting a result, not for any other reason."

"Well you'd better start to think . . . your only way out of this might just be by fingering the real culprit."

He looked at his watch and got up hurriedly, "I have to go, I'm in court shortly and I have to call at the office first." She walked with him to the door. "I'll call you as soon as I get copies of the statements . . . pity you don't know the PIN number or you could get them yourself." She wasn't sure if he was joking or not and her face must have said as much because he smiled at her and said,

"Only kidding" before giving her a peck on the cheek and hurrying off down the path.

Grace stood at the door as he drove away and saw Dermot parking in the space that Andrew had just vacated. She waited for him to come up the path. Anxiously she wondered if he knew, and if he did, what would he say.

"Power's still in a coma," he said.

"What about Ann?"

"Much the same." He walked past her into the kitchen. "I'm going back to James's, do you want to come?"

"You haven't heard then," she said and told him of the morning's events.

He stood listening, his face becoming stony. "Who made the allegation?" he asked.

"Anonymous," she said. "But it's obvious why it's been made."

"Is it?" he said stiffly.

Grace was shocked, she had taken it for granted that Dermot would be on her side and his bullish attitude upset her. "Of course it's obvious, I've been set up. Surely you don't think . . . "

"I'd better go," he said, turning on his heel and heading for the hall. "Dermot?" she called after him, but he just carried on out of the front door and the cold realisation dawned on her that, in the eyes of her colleagues, she now had the plague and any association could leave them open to infection.

Chapter Ten

Tony Farrell's blood test results confirmed that he was indeed an 'A' secretor and the subsequent PGM enzyme test which breaks people down to ten distinct groups, further confirmed that there was a one-in-five chance that Farrell was the last person to have had sexual relations with Nicky and was therefore the prime suspect in her murder.

Later that evening when Forensic found fibres from Nicky's sweat-shirt on an old sheet in the boot of Farrell's car along with smears of blood and semen, he was charged with rape and murder.

Afterwards in Smyths Dermot, Jack Mulloy and Kate O'Grady were in subdued mood.

"Well I don't believe it," said Kate for the fifth time. "Grace was the first one to voice what we were all thinking."

"What better way to avert suspicion?" said Jack. "Get everyone looking in the opposite direction. And why was she so determined that the grandfather was the villain when it was obvious after the tapes that Farrell was the one . . . What d'you think, Dermot?"

Dermot sighed. "What do I think? . . . I think it's hard to believe, but then I can't think of anyone in the unit I'd point the finger at and it has to be someone . . . No one outside knew about the raids . . . and the McDowells knew we were coming." They all nodded silently in reluctant agreement, looking into their drinks to avoid looking at each other.

Hugh O'Boyle came in and after he had bought himself a pint he wandered over. "What's up?" he said. "We're supposed to be celebrating . . . Farrell's banged up, strike one to Harcourt Terrace!"

"Piss off, O'Boyle!" said Kate. "What about poor Grace . . . I don't feel like celebrating while she's . . . "

"I wouldn't cry for yer woman de Rossa . . . It's the ones like her give us all a bad name," O'Boyle said. "Come on lads . . . What're ye drinkin'?"

Dermot knocked back his pint. "I'm off," he said. "I want to see the football."

Kate followed suit and picked up her coat. "Can you drop me?" she asked and Dermot nodded.

"Well suit yerselves," said O'Boyle sounding miffed, and Jack said, "Mine's a Guinness."

Grace was still in a state of shock. Simple tasks were taking an inordinate amount of time because she couldn't concentrate. Andrew had asked her to draw up a list of her shifts and her whereabouts for the last two months but she kept loosing track of where she was up to.

Halfway through the afternoon she decided to take a break and went for a walk in St Stephen's Green. She sat by the lake and watched the baby ducks, nearly forgetting about her problems. At about five it started to turn chilly so she headed back home.

The phone rang at about nine. It was Kathleen. "Grace dear, I have to tell you. The whore . . . "

"Not now, Kathleen," Grace said more sharply than she intended. "I've other problems to sort out."

"What problems, dear?" said the mother-in-law-from-hell rather too sweetly. Grace regretted giving her the opening.

"Just stuff to do with work, Kathleen, nothing you can help me with." But Kathleen refused to be put off.

"Why don't you come round for Sunday lunch, dear . . . put your problems behind you . . . Andrew will be there on his own." Adding by way of explanation, "It's his birthday. Remember?"

"Yes, I remember," she said flatly.

"Good . . . so you'll come then?"

Will she never give up? Grace thought to herself but said aloud, "I don't think so, Kathleen, but thanks for asking." Not to be put off Kathleen went on, "If you don't mind me saying so, Grace, faint heart never won fair lady . . . if you know what I mean?"

"No, Kathleen, I've no idea what you mean."

"Well eh . . . I mean that if you eh . . . give up on Andrew . . . em . . . you'll never win him back."

Grace snapped. "Look Kathleen . . . I wouldn't take back your big girl's blouse of a son if he went down on his bended knees, which is highly improbable seeing as he's quite happy where he is. Please just mind your own business will you, and leave me alone."

The ensuing stunned silence at the other end of the line plunged Grace into an instant guilt trip. Finally Kathleen found her voice and squeaked tearfully, "I only want what's best for you both." And burst into tears before the line went dead.

"*Shit! Shit! Shit!*" Grace yelled at the ceiling. "I really don't need this." Her roar terrified Theo the cat who was sleeping at the foot of the stairs. He leapt up, knocking over an overgrown tree-ivy which engulfed Grace as she attempted to stop it from crashing to the ground. She staggered back, dragging the phone off the table and stepped on the frightened moggy who did a vertical take-off, planted his claws in the back of Grace's legs and hung on for dear life. Grace screamed in pain and the cat took off again, up her back and into the plant. The resulting extra weight caused plant, cat and Grace to clatter backwards onto the floor. The fall knocked the breath out of her and she lay there tangled in jungle foliage, telephone wire and irate feline.

Someone leaned on the doorbell and Grace struggled up to answer it. "OK, OK," she shouted at the back of the door as she endeavoured to free herself. "I'm coming . . . don't get your knickers in a twist."

Phoebe Lamplighter was standing on the doorstep, leaning on the doorbell looking livid and dirty. Just behind her elbow stood a gorilla.

"Phoebe! What're you doing here?" The sight of Grace, entangled in ivy, dragging the phone along the floor left Phoebe open-mouthed. After a moment however she regained her voice and started on a tirade aimed at Grace. "How could you tell them . . . how could you grass me up to them, and why? That's what I want to know . . . What did I ever do to you?"

Grace unwound the ivy leaves and threw them on the floor. "What are you talking about Phoebe? Why are you yelling at me? . . . How did you know my address . . . and who's that?" she said pointing at the gorilla.

Phoebe looked over her shoulder. "That's Mungo," she said. "And stop changing the subject. McDowell's after my blood because you couldn't keep your bloody big stupid mouth shut, so what are you going to do about it?"

"You'd better come in." She stood back and Phoebe and Mungo walked past her into the hall where Mungo proceeded to rescue the distressed plant.

"I've been fire-bombed out of house and home. It's a wonder we weren't killed," Phoebe said.

"That's terrible, but why are you taking it out on me? I certainly didn't talk to Branden McDowell."

"Then how did he know that I was the one who told you about his venture into film if you didn't tell him?"

"Not you too!" Grace said wearily, sinking down onto the bottom step of the stairs with her head in her hands. "Who said I told him?"

Surprised at Grace's reaction Phoebe calmed down. "I don't mean *you* particularly . . . by *you*, I mean the gardaí in general, Harcourt Terrace specifically."

Grace looked over at Mungo, who was still fiddling with the plant. "Who's Mungo?" she mouthed, inclining her head at the huge giant of a man. He was black, all of six feet six inches tall and built like a granite monument. His head was shaved and shiny. His muscles bulged through his ill-fitting jacket but he handled the delicate plant as gently as if it were a baby.

"Mungo's my chauffeur," Phoebe said. "If it wasn't for him I'd be dead, he got me out of the fire fairly unscathed, which is more than I can say about the house. It's completely gutted . . . have you got a cigarette?"

"I gave up . . . You say it was Branden McDowell?"

Phoebe sighed. "Well . . . one of his minions, but I know he arranged it . . . you can bet your life . . . So what are you going to do about it?"

Grace snorted. "There's not much I can do about it. He's just about finished me off too."

Phoebe looked at her, a puzzled expression on her face. "What are you talking about?"

Grace proceeded to tell her of the set-up and of Killery's visit that morning.

"So who do you think set you up?"

Grace shrugged. "Your guess is a good as mine," she said. "But it doesn't take a mastermind to figure out that we're both looking for the same person."

Mungo, who had finished fixing the plant, looked over at Phoebe. "I think you should stay here. McDowell won't look for you here." He had a quiet voice with a soft American accent, but also the sort of tone people aren't generally prepared to argue with.

81

Phoebe nodded and got to her feet. "Good point," she said before Grace could answer. "He'll go crazy when he discovers I'm not a kebab yet . . . what do you think, de Rossa?"

"What d'you mean . . . stay here?"

"Well, what do you think I mean? We've nowhere else to go tonight, all my credit cards, cash and cheque book went up with the house . . . by the way I'd kill for a bath, and have you any clean clothes I could borrow until I can go shopping . . . all mine were destroyed in the fire?" She stood up and headed for the stairs. "Up here, is it?"

"It would be best," Mungo said quietly and Grace reluctantly agreed, not having the energy to argue.

"I'll find you something to wear," she said, sounding resigned, and followed Phoebe up the stairs.

"I'm sorry to impose," Phoebe said as Grace opened the wardrobe. "But look at it this way, you get a temporary minder at the same time, and between us we might be able to find out which bastard has sold us out."

Grace didn't answer and started to root through the wardrobe for something to fit Phoebe, who was smaller and a good bit slimmer than she was. Suddenly a pair of very high, exorbitantly expensive, sexy red Italian shoes caught her eye, neatly lined up with her other shoes at the bottom of the wardrobe.

"Someone's been in here!" she exclaimed, grabbing the shoes. "These were in a box . . . I left them in the box." She knelt down and dragged out the shoe-box which was stacked with three others at the back of the wardrobe. Hands shaking, she ripped off the lid and whipped back the black tissue paper.

Phoebe, who was looking over her shoulder gave a low whistle. "Must be two grand there at least," she said looking at the neatly stacked twenty pound notes nestling in the bottom of the box.

Grace felt panic rising in her chest but she managed

to subdue it. "Quick!" she said rummaging in the chest of drawers and pulling out an old grey track suit. "Put this on . . . I've got to get this money out of the house. Whoever put it here will have tipped off Killery about it." Phoebe was holding the track suit at arms length with a disgusted look on her face. "Come on Phoebe . . . put it on . . . take the money out of here."

"Where?"

"For God's sake, Phoebe, anywhere . . . I don't care, just get it out of here." Grace found a plastic bag and packed the notes inside replacing the shoes in the box and stacking them neatly. Phoebe, who managed to look ravishing in the old track suit, was struggling into a pair of Grace's trainers.

Back downstairs in the kitchen Mungo had made a pot of tea. "Milk and sugar?" he said to Grace as she hurried into the kitchen closely followed by Phoebe.

"I don't think there's time, thank you, Mungo," she said agitated.

But Phoebe said, "Thank you, Mungo . . . I'd kill for a cuppa."

"Phoebe . . . Please . . . " said Grace in desperation just as the doorbell rang again. The three of them froze. "That'll be Killery!" exclaimed Grace.

Mungo gently took Phoebe's arm and picked up the plastic bag stuffing it down the top of his trousers. "C'mon," he said to Phoebe and led her to the back door. "We'll be back later," he said as the two of them disappeared into the darkness.

Grace picked up the phone on her way through the hall to answer the door. Killery barged past her and went straight upstairs.

"What d'you want now?" she shouted after him.

"Sorry," said Declan as he too pushed past her and followed his Inspector. Grace caught up with them as they reached the landing.

"Which room's yours?" Killery asked gruffly.

Grace pushed open the door of her bedroom. "You should know," she said. "You've wrecked it once already today."

He went straight to the wardrobe as she knew he would and pulled out the shoe-boxes, emptying the contents on to the bed.

"Watch those!" she shouted as the red shoes hit the duvet. "They're new . . . What are you looking for?"

Killery looked round at her. "I think you know the answer to that," he said. "Where is it?"

"Where's what . . . what are you talking about?"

Killery looked at Declan and they proceeded to tear the room apart again. "I just finished cleaning this lot up from this morning," she said. "You couldn't possibly have missed anything."

"Our information says different," Killery said. They left an hour later after Grace, who was more in control on this occasion, had self-righteously insisted that they tidy up after themselves.

Phoebe and Mungo arrived back soon after.

"What did you do with the money?" Grace asked as they drank the fresh tea that Mungo had insisted on making.

"The monks at St Teresa's got an early Easter present," Phoebe said.

Grace made up the bed in the spare room for Phoebe but Mungo insisted on dozing on the couch in the living-room. Later, after her bath, Phoebe joined Grace in the kitchen. Her wet hair was wrapped in a towel, her face devoid of make-up and she had found Andrew's old dressing-gown, but despite this, she once again looked gorgeous.

"You know we have to bring down Branden McDowell," she said with an air of seriousness.

Grace burst out laughing. "What's this *we*? . . . What

makes you think the two of us can do what the entire Garda Síochána and all of its resources have miserably failed to achieve despite their best efforts?"

"First of all," said Phoebe, settling down at the table, "we have a secret weapon."

"Which is?"

"Mungo of course . . . and we don't have to follow the letter of the law do we? What the eye doesn't see and all that."

"Give me a break, Phoebe! I'm an officer of the court, I have to be seen to follow the letter of the law."

It was Phoebe's turn to laugh, she threw back her head and guffawed. "You won't be an officer of the court for much longer if we can't sort this little spot of bother out." Grace had to concede that she had a point.

"I bet if we could get in to Branden's on Fenian Street and go through the records, we'd find some pretty incriminating stuff."

"What makes you think they keep the records in the snooker club?"

"That's where McDowell took Seán Platt when they were talking about the film. He told me Branden had a state of the art computer system to keep all his interests organised . . . Branden fancies himself as a bit of a computer buff. Anyway he was bragging to Seán about the system. Needless to say the stupid little prat was suitably impressed."

"How would we get into the system? I don't know about you, but I know the minimum about computers bar operating the system at work."

"Don't worry about that," said Phoebe with a smug look on her face. "There are a few favours I can call in that will sort out that little problem."

They sat in silence on either side of the kitchen table and it suddenly struck Grace how quickly life can turn around. The last thing she had expected was to be relying on a high-class hooker and a hard-man to help her to hold on to both her career and her liberty.

The following morning when she got up she found that Phoebe and Mungo had already left the house. She found a note on the kitchen table. *Back later* was all it said.

Chapter Eleven

At about the same time as Grace was reading Phoebe's note, O'Keefe called Dermot to his office.

"We have a problem," he said and handed Dermot a typed lab report. "It seems that although Farrell has the same blood group and PGM as the last man to have had carnal knowledge of the victim, the DNA fingerprint makes it ninety-nine point nine percent certain that he was not that person."

"But he admitted having sex with the girl."

"I know, that's as may be, but he must have used a condom because he definitely wasn't the last person to go with her."

Dermot was stunned. "Are they sure?"

O'Keefe nodded. "If you read down a bit you'll see the other conclusions."

Dermot's eyes scanned down the page. "Jesus!" he exclaimed.

"Exactly my reaction," said O'Keefe. "The DNA of the victim and the perpetrator are as close a match as it's possible to get. Nicky's own father raped and probably killed her."

"And the tissue type of the foetus makes another match. Christ! what a mess."

"To put it mildly," said O'Keefe. "What did Ann Power say about Nicky's father?"

"Nothing, but Leonard Power told de Rossa that he didn't know who the father was and that the father didn't even know of her existence."

"It'd be a million to one chance of Nicky meeting her father by chance, let alone of him raping her."

"Nicky's mother has to know who the father is even if Leonard Power doesn't . . . and what about Assumpta Power, maybe she knows."

"Go and see. Now, what are we going to do about Tony Farrell, his brief'll make a meal out of this."

Dermot shrugged. "We had good grounds to charge him with the murder. I dare say he'll be relieved to only be charged with having sex with a minor." He handed the lab report back to O'Keefe and was just about to leave when a thought struck him. "What about Philo Hoban's assertion that the grandfather was abusing Nicky . . . if that were true the odds would be firmly in favour of his having abused Ann. He could be Nicky's father."

"It's a possibility, but at the moment there's not much chance of the hospital letting us near him so we'll have to leave that on hold for the moment. Go and talk to Assumpta Power and see what she says, but first go and break the good news to Tony Farrell."

"Thanks a bunch, boss!" he said and went to collect Jack Mulloy. He could have that pleasure instead.

Assumpta Power received Dermot in the front drawing-room. She was sitting by a huge fire with a tea tray across the arm rests of her wheelchair. "Would you like a cup, sergeant?" she asked.

"Thank you," he said and sat opposite her. She proceeded to pour tea into a fine bone china cup and handed it to him. She had added milk without consulting him.

"Sugar?" she asked, and he shook his head and took

the cup from her hand.

"Mrs Power, I have to ask you a few questions concerning your daughter."

Her friendly manner turned instantly frosty. "I have no daughter," she snapped.

Dermot tried again. "Mrs Power. Ann, your daughter, had a child some fourteen years ago. Do you know who the father was?"

Assumpta Power set her jaw and glared at Dermot. "Please . . . It's very important . . . If we're to catch the killer."

"Killer? . . . What killer? . . . What are you talking about?" she said and Dermot realised that she still didn't know about her granddaughter's death.

"Nicky was murdered. Didn't your husband tell you?" Assumpta's face was ashen.

"Dead? . . . Dead?" she kept repeating. "Who killed her?"

"The lab results strongly suggest that her own father, whoever he is, was the murderer."

"How can they know that?" she asked, still dazed.

"Because she was raped before she was strangled . . . I'm sorry to have to put it so bluntly."

Assumpta seemed to age before his eyes and she slumped into her wheelchair.

"Do you know who Nicky's father is, Mrs Power?" Dermot coaxed.

She looked up with tears in her eyes and nodded. "Yes . . . I know who my granddaughter's father is, may God forgive him." She sat still staring into the fire. Dermot waited for her to gather herself together. "Ann was always a difficult child . . . The devil was in her."

"What do you mean?" Dermot said, perplexed by her choice of language. Assumpta's mouth was set into a thin line as she spoke of her daughter, her hands clenched in her lap. "She was a temptress, a Jezebel. Always flaunting herself in front of men."

Dermot found it hard to believe that this bitter old crow was talking about the nervous mousy woman he knew as Ann Power. And he had difficulty in keeping a straight face when she used the archaic and inappropriate name.

"A slut of the first order," she said adding weight to her opinion. Dermot waited for her to elaborate but she stayed silent.

Eventually he said, "Why do you say that?"

Assumpta Power sniffed then said, "She always acted strangely. I did my best to bring her up fearing God. She heard Mass every morning, always did the nine first Fridays. The only explanation for her was that she was an aberration, a devil child . . . conceived in lust." She spat out the last sentence, averting her eyes from him. Again there was a long silence.

Dermot was losing patience. "About the man who made her pregnant?"

"Humph . . . Another agent of the devil! . . . His name was Jerome Proudfoot."

"You said *was*. Is he dead?"

"I have no idea, but I truly hope so."

Again she was silent, staring into the fire. Suddenly she turned to him and said, "Jerome Proudfoot was a handyman gardener who used to work for my husband. She bewitched him. Then her belly started to swell and I knew what they had been at." She paused as if trying to recall events. "I made her confess her sin . . . I beat her to purge her guilt . . . I made her fast and pray for forgiveness."

"Did she tell you that Jerome Proudfoot was the father of her baby?" Dermot asked through gritted teeth. With a mother like Assumpta he wasn't surprised that Ann was such a nervous wreck.

"She didn't need to . . . I knew . . . I saw her looking at

90

him . . . devouring him with her eyes."

"What became of him, do you know where he is now?" he asked, knowing what her answer would be.

"I hope he's burning in hell, the fornicator." The woman was giving him the creeps, the hate in the room was palpable.

"I need to know where he came from, if he has any family, where they live now if he has?" he said, trying to keep his temper. Leonard Power's wife wheeled her chair towards the door and opened it. "Maude," she called, and Dermot heard the housekeeper's shoes squeaking down the hall.

"Yes Mam?" she said with such deference he was surprised that she didn't drop a curtsey.

"Garda Sergeant McEvoy wants to know about the Proudfoot person." She said it with a sneer in her voice, and wheeled herself out into the hall closing the door behind her.

Maude was plump and in her early sixties. She had worked for Assumpta's family since girlhood, the house in Park Avenue being Assumpta's family home. She stood by the door her hands clasped behind her back waiting for Dermot to speak to her. "What can you tell me about Jerome Proudfoot, Maude?" She shifted from one foot to the other.

"He used to work for Mr Leonard, in the garden and so forth."

"And?"

She shrugged. "What's to say? His mother still lives in the village I think, Seafort Avenue. After Miss Ann got into trouble and they sent her to the home he ran off. The missus said he was the father."

"Do you know where he went?"

Maude shook her head. "I wouldn't know, but it was the talk of the village at the time. His ma never believed that Miss Ann had the baby for him, though I'm sure it was him. Who else would it be? Sure she never went anywhere . . . where would she meet anyone else?" She stopped, fearing she had said too much. She had a worried look on her face. "You won't tell the missus I said that, will you? About her not meetin' anyone else."

Dermot assured her that anything she had to say would be treated in confidence. Maude folded her arms across her ample bosom. She looked furtively over her shoulder towards the hall. "I felt sorry for her. Twenty-eight years of age and she wasn't let have a job or friends of her own." Maude indicated the hall with her head. "She beat her with a rod on the bare back when she started to show, and her a grown woman."

"What did you think of Proudfoot?"

Maude shrugged. "Nice enough boy, he was a couple of years younger than Miss Ann, but not very bright . . . a bit slow if you know what I mean."

"Why did she never come home again after she had the baby?"

"*She* wouldn't have anything to do with her. I think Mr Leonard looked after her though, unbeknown to the missus."

Dermot left without speaking to Assumpta Power again and headed round to Seafort Avenue. After knocking on a few doors he finally found the Proudfoot residence.

Della Phillips was Jerome's sister. She didn't have many kind words to say about Assumpta Power or her husband and had no idea where her brother was. It transpired in the course of the conversation that she blamed her brother for their mother's premature death. Before he left her, Dermot managed to borrow a fifteen-year-old studio photograph of her errant brother. When he got back to Harcourt Square the picture together with a request for information was faxed to every garda station in the State.

Grace didn't want to leave the house empty, she feared what she, or rather Killery, might find on her return. The morning was endless and she spent the time finishing off her list of duties for Andrew. He called round just before eleven to collect it. He was in a hurry and she thought his attitude was rather offhand when she told him about finding the one hundred twenty pound notes hidden in the bottom of her wardrobe. It was only when Phoebe entered the equation that he hit the roof.

"Are you crazy?" he yelled. "Are you out of your mind? Letting a known prostitute not only sleep in your house but conspiring with her to destroy evidence! Where's your brain, woman?"

Grace was speechless for a moment until she suddenly realised what he was really saying. "You arrogant prick!" she shouted back. "How dare you lecture me. What did you expect me to do? Let Killery find the money and then hold up my hands in surprise and say how did that get there? Get real, Andrew, some bent bastard's trying to set me up and I'm not about to sit back and let it happen."

"The end justifies the means . . . is that what you're saying?" he said, standing feet planted apart, hands on his hips.

"For God's sake don't be so melodramatic, Andrew, you'd think I was responsible for the Holocaust the way you're talking. Anyway what happened to the principle of innocent until proven guilty? Phoebe's never been convicted of prostitution in this country, and it seems to me she's being a lot more constructive than you are."

They stood staring each other out, both fuming until Andrew slapped the list of duties on the kitchen table along with the computer printout of the building society withdrawals. "If that's the way you want it . . . fine," he said. "Let your new friend sort this lot out. I wash my hands of you."

"Thank you, Pontius Pilate!" she screamed at his back as he stormed out of the front door, slamming it after him.

It took her twenty minutes to calm down enough to start comparing the two lists and she found that of the ten transactions made by cash card, there were only two occasions where she could prove her whereabouts. All of the transactions were from city branches, and she was astounded to note that approximately five thousand pounds had gone through the account in the past year, not counting the two thousand of the previous evening. She tried to think of any member of the unit who had money troubles. That led nowhere. Everyone she knew, including herself, had money troubles. The obvious thing was to think of someone who didn't have money problems, so she made a list of all her colleagues. She put a line through Dermot's name for obvious reasons. Even if he was corrupt, and she didn't think he was, he wouldn't deal with the McDowells. Jack Mulloy never seemed to be particularly flush but he was never skint either, even though two of his children were at collage. She knew Hugh was fond of a bet on the horses and liked to drink too much, but then his wife had a good job in the civil service and they had no family to put through third level education. Kate, well there was no way . . .

The door bell announced Phoebe and Mungo's return so she put her list to one side. Mungo was laden with black Brown Thomas bags and Phoebe floated past on a waft of Eternity wearing new Levi's, leather biker's jacket and emerald Gucci loafers.

"You look as if you lost fifty quid and found a parking ticket," she said on the way past. "Lighten up."

Chapter Twelve

Mungo went out at about seven that evening to collect Phoebe's other secret weapon.

"Who is this computer buff anyway?" Grace asked.

Phoebe, who was painting her nails, looked up and said, "Ronan."

"Yes . . . but who *is* Ronan? . . . What have you got on him that he'll risk helping us?"

"He's not helping us, he's helping me," she said with an air of high dudgeon. "And I haven't got anything on him, as you put it." She went back to painting her nails.

Grace switched on the television but found it hard to concentrate. She had been cooped up in the house all day and was feeling edgy. By nine, when Mungo hadn't returned, she said to Phoebe. "Maybe he won't do it, maybe Mungo couldn't persuade him. He's been gone a long time."

"Don't fret," was her answer. "They'll be here soon."

Just after ten they heard Mungo at the door and Phoebe went out to answer it. He walked in followed by a spotty youth of about twelve, dressed in school uniform. To Grace's further amazement Phoebe hugged the boy, who was obviously pleased to see her.

"Grace, I'd like you to meet Ronan," she said and turned to the boy. "This is Grace de Rossa, Ronan."

The youth, who was slight and pasty-faced stepped

forward and formally shook hands with Grace. "How do you do?" he said. He had a nondescript, unidentifiable accent.

"You made good time," Phoebe said to Mungo.

"The roads were empty once I got into Kildare," he said and headed for the kitchen carrying Ronan's sports bag. "I'll fix him somethin' to eat."

Grace watched all this in bewilderment and after Ronan had followed Mungo through to the kitchen she grabbed Phoebe's arm to hold her back. "Who's the kid . . . what's he doing here?"

Phoebe lifted Grace's hand off her arm. "Relax . . . he's my son."

Now Grace was even more perplexed. "What's your son doing here?" She hadn't even been aware that Phoebe had a son.

"Ronan's my expert witness. What he doesn't know about computers isn't worth knowing."

"But he's only a kid. How can you let him take the risk?"

From being light-hearted Phoebe turned deadly serious. "At the risk of being melodramatic," she said in a low intense voice, "I don't have a choice. He may not have a mother if McDowell isn't put away, and I for one don't want him orphaned just yet."

"But I thought you had favours to call in? Why d'you need to use Ronan?"

"As I said . . . I haven't a choice. If you must know, no one came across for me," Phoebe said sullenly and walked past her into the kitchen.

Grace followed and sat at the table next to Ronan. "Well, Ronan, so you know about computers?" she said trying to make conversation while Mungo clattered about at the cooker.

"You could say that," Ronan said. "I'm evolving a virus disguised as a fantasy game at the moment. The punch comes at the end when the player reaches the final level."

"Oh?" she said, mystified.

"Yes . . . when they reach the end of the game their hard disk self-destructs," he said and became helpless with mirth.

"Oh," Grace said again, and caught Phoebe gazing proudly at the boy, her expression clearly said that's my son.

Just after one in the morning Grace parked in Denzille Lane and she, the hooker, the hard-man and the kid stumbled along by the reflected light from the street-lights in Fenian Street, looking for the rear entry to Branden's snooker club. *What the hell am I doing here?* she thought. Aloud she said, "It should be about here." She stopped by a tall wooden gate. Phoebe shone her torch over the peeling paint looking for some sign that they were indeed in the right place.

"No. It's this one," Mungo said in a low voice from a few feet down the lane. Phoebe jumped, dropping the torch with a clatter.

"Shhhhh!" hissed Grace and they all froze. The bright lights in Fenian Street made the roof appear in silhouette and they could see that it was four storeys at the back even though Grace knew that the front rose to only three. A small door was set into the gate and she rattled it as quietly as she could to see if it was locked. It failed to give way and she felt Mungo's hand on her arm.

"Let me," he said and shone his own pencil torch on the Yale, proceeding to fiddle with a set of picks. He selected one and manipulated it in the lock. Seconds later it clicked and the door gave way.

Grace cautiously stepped through the opening followed closely by Phoebe and Ronan. Mungo brought up the rear. Suddenly, from the far corner of the yard, came the sound of a low rumbling growl which grew in intensity to a snarl. Grace stopped dead and Phoebe bumped into her back.

"What's that?" she hissed and shone her torch in the direction of the noise. It illuminated two yellow eyes and a set of very large ivory teeth. Suddenly all hell broke loose and the huge black shape started to bark, snarl and growl, building up to a frenzy. It crouched ready to spring, in the beam of the torch. They stood frozen to the spot like rabbits caught in the headlamps, then turned and fled just as the beast sprang, lurching to a halt as it reached the limit of it's chain.

"Shit! I hate dogs!" Grace panted, her back against the gate. "We'll just have to revert to plan B."

"Which is?" Phoebe said and Grace gave her a weary look.

Leaving the car in the lane, they made their way round in ragged procession to Fenian Street and stopped in front of Branden's. The whole place was in darkness as were the adjacent buildings. Mungo tackled the front door lock as quickly and efficiently as he had a few minutes before, which left Grace in little doubt as to what his occupation had been before he had become Phoebe's chauffeur.

He crossed the threshold first and the others followed. The air smelt of stale beer and even staler cigarette smoke. On the right of the front door was a set of glass-panelled double doors leading into the snooker room and at the end of the hall, through an arch, was a wide staircase.

"Where does he keep the computer system?" Grace asked. Mungo, who was by this time half way up the first flight, said, "Seán Platt says top floor." He ran up the stairs two at a time. Grace couldn't believe how light on his feet and agile he was. By the time the two women and the boy caught up with him on the top landing he was already working on the door lock.

Phoebe leaned against the wall to get her breath. Grace held the torch for Mungo. The lock was old and awkward and took some time.

Phoebe got impatient. "Come on, Mungo, get a move on," she said.

Mungo turned and held the thin piece of metal out to her. "You wanna do it?" he said sarcastically but she pursed her lips and shook her head. He went back to the job in hand, and moments later there was a click and he turned the aged brass knob and pushed the door open. Grace shone the torch round the room. It was cluttered with cartons of cigarettes and drink but there was no sign of any computer or even a desk. "Shit!" said Mungo. "Must be the next room." And he pushed past Phoebe and tried the door which, as it turned out, wasn't even locked.

The beam from Phoebe's torch reflected off a computer screen. "Eureka!" she said.

Ronan went over to it, testing the on-off switch. "An APS Bravo 323," he said. "Good, not bad, but hardly state of the art." The screen lit up and he punched a few of the keys on the keyboard and sat waiting. "Look round for any three-and-a-half-inch disks you can find," he said over his shoulder. As Phoebe and Grace searched in the desk drawers Mungo said, "I'll keep an eye on the front door," and left the room.

The room was furnished as an office with desk, filing cabinets and shelving, but there was also a long overstuffed sofa along one wall and a gas fire set into the cast-iron fireplace.

"What d'you think this McDowell chap would use as a password, Phoebe?" Ronan said after a while. "I've tried all the obvious ones, and I can't get into the system."

"I thought you said there was nothing the kid didn't know about computers," Grace hissed under her breath.

Phoebe ignored the remark and said to the boy, "I'd say he's the type to use something twee like Mother or Ma . . . What's his mother's name, Grace? . . . Does he have a dog or anything . . . well apart from Cuddles downstairs?"

Grace thought for a moment. "His mother's called Sarah and I'd say the dog would be called something affectionate like Killer or Fang," she said half-heartedly, her instincts concerning the futility of the operation being reinforced by the minute. *He's only just switched the bloody thing on and he's stuck,* she thought to herself.

"I'm in!" Ronan suddenly exclaimed and Phoebe gave Grace an I-told-you-so look. "The password's Mum," he said in disgust. "What d'you you want me to look for?"

"Anything to do with accounts or payments, or anything that looks iffy," Grace said standing behind him watching the screen. They looked at the directory, scanning the names of the files, and Ronan accessed any that Grace thought might be relevant. After an hour it was obvious that all the files in the permanent hard disk memory were bona fide files for the tax man and they found not the slightest thing that could be regarded as incriminating.

"Pity he's not as daft as his password would suggest," Ronan said. "There must be some disks somewhere, look again."

Phoebe and Grace resumed the search and ten minutes later Grace found a box of disks on the top of a stack of metal shelving, pushed to the back.

"Let's try these," she said triumphantly, and flipped through the contents of the box, reading the labels. "They're all in a code of some sort," she said and picking one at random she pushed it into the disk drive.

"Let's take a look at this one."

The disk contained a spreadsheet with lists of businesses along the top and dates and payments down the side. Grace scanned along the list. All of the addresses were on the south side of the city and the payments appeared to be weekly. One address caught her eye and she started to laugh. "Brilliant!" she burst out. "This has to be a list of his protection rackets. Look at this one." She pointed to an address in The Coombe which had obviously ceased payments. After the fourth missed payment the word terminate was entered. Grace knew that this particular carpet warehouse had been burnt out on that date and arson was suspected.

"Can you put this on a split screen with the Feel Safe Security file that's on the hard disk?"

"I'd have to copy this floppy disk onto the hard disk first," Ronan said and typed in a command. When the two files were up on the screen side by side it was clear that Feel Safe was indeed a front for the extortion racket as they had suspected. Both files were identical in every detail except for the cash amounts which were much more substantial on the protection racket file.

"Right let's get out of here," said Phoebe, sounding relieved.

"Hang on a minute," said Grace. "There might be enough to put McDowell away on the disk but it doesn't solve my little problem, does it?"

Phoebe, who was standing by the door, laughed. "Of course it does. If you take this in to your Inspector surely it proves you couldn't possibly be involved with the McDowells."

Grace heaved a sigh. "Phoebe, if I take that disk in, the only thing it proves is that I'm guilty of breaking and entering, or worse that I fabricated the whole thing. We've no proof that it came from here, or any hint who's taking the shilling from your friend Branden."

"She's right, Phoebe," Ronan said. "We need to see if any of the other disks give a hint about the bent copper. My guess is this idiot has records of everything, and if we can find the right disks and hide them somewhere in this building, where the McDowells can't find them, Grace can tip off her garda friends, and they can get a search warrant and discover them." Ronan was growing in Grace's estimation by the minute.

"Couldn't we copy the disks?" Phoebe asked.

"If we had blanks we could," the boy said. "But I didn't bring any. We could always come back and do it I suppose."

"No chance!" Grace burst out. "Let's just look through the other disks and see what's on them. I want out of here as soon as possible."

After looking at three equally incriminating files Phoebe was ecstatic and Grace was sinking further into despair. There was nothing referring to pay-offs to the gardaí. Ronan was just slipping another disk into the drive when Mungo appeared at the door.

"Someone's just pulled up outside!" he said softly making them jump. "We'd better get outta here."

Ronan clicked off the computer and Grace grabbed the disks and frantically looked for somewhere to hide them. "Come on!" urged Mungo.

"I have to hide these somewhere," she said, her eyes darting round the room.

Mungo grabbed the disks from her hand. "We haven't time for that," he said. "Hurry up!" Phoebe was already on the landing with Ronan when, from down below, they all heard the front door being opened. Mungo pushed the door of the store room. "In here," he ordered and they scuttled quickly inside.

Then Grace remembered that there was still the disk that Ronan had just placed in the disk drive. She poked her head out of the store room door but pulled back quickly when she heard footsteps on the stairs below. "Shit! they're coming up here," she hissed, crouching down behind the cigarette cartons beside Phoebe and Ronan. Mungo had flattened himself (as much as a hulk can flatten himself) behind the door.

They all held their breath as the voices came closer and the footsteps started to climb the final flight. A male voice said something indistinguishable and a young female voice answered then screeched with laughter. Grace strained her ears, and as they reached the landing she recognised Alan McDowell's voice.

"I told yeh I'd look after yeh, didn't I," he said. "C'mon in here and yeh can thank me properly."

The girl giggled and said. "Now, Alan, yeh said there'd be none of that . . . " Grace recognised Philo Hoban's voice as they walked past the store room. The door of the office opened and closed and then she heard more muffled laughter. A few moments later one of them must have switched on a radio because music filtered through the walls along with the hum of conversation.

"My leg's going to sleep," Phoebe whispered, shifting where she crouched to try and ease it. "D'you think it's safe to make a move yet?" Grace put her finger to her lips and shook her head.

After fifteen minutes all feeling had left Phoebe's legs and she tried to rub some life back into them, only succeeding in stimulating excruciating pins and needles. She winced. *What the hell am I doing here?* she thought to herself, reflecting that a few short years before she had been, as she thought, set up for life. Now here she was hiding in a rundown snooker club, relying on a not very bright policewoman, whom she didn't particularly like, to prevent her from being carved up by a pair of twopenny-halfpenny gangsters. She looked across to where Grace was crouched with her ear against the wall of the adjoining room and gingerly started rubbing some life back into her legs again. Little did she know that Grace was having the very same reservations about her own situation.

A little later, when the conversation in the next room ceased but the music continued, Grace tapped Mungo on the arm. "I don't think Alan McDowell'll be in any position to come after us if we go now," she whispered, and he nodded in agreement. Phoebe limped after them, pushing Ronan gently ahead of her. When they were all on the landing near the top of the stairs, Mungo stopped dead. Someone was downstairs in the hall, making for the stairs. He turned and signalled to the women and the boy to head for the fire escape at the far end of the corridor.

"Who's up there?" a voice shouted. Throwing caution to the wind they all pelted past the office to the fire door. Mungo reached it first and wrenched it open and the cold night air hit them in the face. Footsteps thumped up the second flight of stairs.

"Who's there . . . Answer me," shouted the voice again.

Grace, who was at the back of the retreat, reached the rickety fire escape just as Alan McDowell, trousers round his knees, flung the office door open and stumbled out onto the landing. Mungo was by this time at the bottom of the iron staircase and the devil dog once again was snarling and barking and straining at its chain. Phoebe skirted the animal, dragging Ronan after her, and when Grace was near the bottom she heard Branden McDowell's voice yelling at his brother and Alan roaring back at him. She leaned her weight on the stair rail and jumped the last four steps, kicking the dog, who had timed its lunge, in the head. It yelped and lurched forward again, but Grace was out of reach by the gate.

She rummaged in her pocket for the car keys as the clatter of two sets of footsteps raced down the iron fire escape after them. She heard the chain clank as the dog was set free. "Get 'em, Tyson," Branden shouted and flung the gate open.

Ronan just managed to slam the car door before the hound threw itself at the side of the vehicle. The weight of the onslaught made the car shudder. Grace turned the ignition key and the engine turned over but didn't start. The beast made another leap, this time landing on the bonnet and it scrabbled at the windscreen.

"Come on, come on . . . start, damn you!" Grace shouted, turning the key frantically. Mercifully the engine sprang to life and with wheels spinning the car took off towards Holles Street. The dog was thrown to the ground and Grace felt a bump as the front wheel went over it. She winced and looked in the rear view mirror where she saw the two McDowells kneeling by the animal in the lane, screaming obscenities after them and shaking their fists.

"D'you think they recognised us?" Phoebe said, looking out of the rear window.

Grace had taken the corner on two wheels and had to swerve to avoid an unsuspecting taxi ambling down Holles Street.

"What do you think?" she answered sarcastically.

It was well after four in the morning when they got back to Grace's house. After Ronan had made tea they all sat round the kitchen table and discussed their options.

"I think the best thing to do is for me to tip off Dermot about the disks so he can get a warrant and go in and get them," Grace said. "Where did you hide them, Mungo?"

Mungo looked uncomfortable. "Hide them?" he said sheepishly. "I thought you needed them for evidence against Branden McDowell."

Three heads turned in his direction and Grace groaned as his huge paw placed the disks in the middle of the table.

"We could always send them to Harcourt Terrace

anonymously," Phoebe volunteered.

"No good," said Ronan. "The evidence was obtained illegally, and as Grace said while we were at the snooker hall, it has to be found on the premises to hold up in court."

Phoebe gave him a withering look. "So what are you saying, Ronan . . . that we have to take the bloody disks back again?"

Ronan shrugged and said, "I suppose so."

They sat dejectedly round the table and the clock in the hall chimed the half hour. Suddenly Phoebe jumped up. "What are we doing sitting here? If Branden McDowell recognised us and finds the disks are missing, he could send his goons round here at any minute."

"Calm down, Phoebe . . . He doesn't know where I live, and I doubt that he's spotted that the disks have gone yet," Grace said.

Mungo agreed with her. "I think we should sleep on it," he said. "I have to get Ronan back to school in a couple of hours and I don't know about you two, but I'm beat."

The sleeping arrangements of the previous night were employed. Ronan shared the sofa bed with Mungo. Grace lay in bed unable to close an eye. Her mind was in turmoil as she went over the events of the past few days. At about five-thirty she finally decided to call Dermot first thing and talk to him. She was afraid to trust anyone else under the circumstances. She drifted off to sleep shortly afterwards.

Chapter Thirteen

Garth Brooks woke Grace the following morning as the radio-alarm blared in her ear. She slapped the snooze button to stop the noise and turned down the volume. She could hear Mungo and Ronan moving about downstairs but Phoebe was still asleep. She reached for the phone and dialled Dermot's extension at Harcourt Terrace. He answered on the second ring. "McEvoy," he said.

"Dermot . . . it's me. I need your help."

There was a sickening silence at the other end of the line, then in a low voice he said, "OK . . . What can I do?"

Still not sure of his attitude towards her she said, "Can we meet somewhere, I have something that can put Branden McDowell away and I don't know who else to trust."

"I don't know," he said.

"Look, Dermot, you know as well as I do that I've been set up." Again there was silence at the other end of the phone. "You want to put Branden away, don't you . . . what have you got to loose?" she pleaded, desperate now.

"OK," he said eventually. "I'll meet you upstairs in the Mary Street Bewley's in twenty minutes," and rang off.

Phoebe reluctantly agreed to stay in the house on guard duty and Mungo was just setting off to take Ronan back to school as she left the house. The traffic was heavy but she made it into town on time but was on her second mug of coffee before she saw Dermot walking over to join her.

"I was afraid you weren't coming," she said, relieved to see him as he sat down opposite her.

He gave her a warm smile and she relaxed a little. "I'm sorry I'm late," he said. "I had to take a call from Mayo. So what's the story?"

"I've come by some computer disks," she started and told him the whole story.

When she had finished he closed his eyes and exhaled loudly. "You know it's inadmissible . . . " he started to say.

"I know, I know," she cut in. "But if you got a warrant you could plant the disks and then find them on the premises quite lawfully, and really Dermot, it's serious stuff, it's the proof that Feel Safe is a front for extortion."

He lit a cigarette and sat staring at her, but she couldn't read his expression. Finally he stubbed out the cigarette and said, "Where are the disks now?"

"Safe."

"Grace, if you don't give them to me I can't find them at Branden's," he said. "So where are they?"

"In a minute," she said. "There's something else." He raised his eyebrows and waited for her to speak. "I want you to tell the rest of the unit that I have the disks."

"Why would I do that? It'd leave you vulnerable to whoever's taking the shilling, they'd tell McDowell."

"I know . . . that's what I want."

"But why for fuck's sake?" he said exasperated.

"Shut up for a minute and I'll tell you," she said full of relief and gratitude that he believed in her. "I intend to call Killery and try and do a deal."

He looked at her suspiciously. "What kind of deal?"

"The only way I can prove that I'm not bent is to trap the bastard who is, so if I can persuade Killery to help I should be off the hook."

"Why should he do a deal with you? He thinks you're guilty?"

"Because you're going to talk him into it," she said, giving him a dazzling smile.

He drummed his fingers on the edge of the table, thinking it through. "OK . . . so I talk him into what?"

"Branden McDowell should soon realise that I've got his disks. What if you tell each member of the unit, separately, and supposedly in confidence, that I've contacted you and that I want to hand them over to you at a specific time and place, a different time and place for everyone of course. Then all Killery has to do is see when and where Branden McDowell turns up."

"I don't understand. What's to stop Killery from thinking that you're setting up an innocent member of the unit for your own ends?"

"Good point," she said. "But only he and you need to know the times and places, then the only way McDowell can find out is via the bent bastard that's trying to bury me."

Dermot looked dubious. "Go and get us another couple of coffees, I want to think about this for a while," he said. "And I'll have a cherry bun while you're at it."

When she returned with the coffee and buns Dermot said, "OK, so Killery turns up at some place and sees Branden waiting supposedly for you to turn up with the disks. What *about* the disks, when do I go in for those? And I hardly think someone from Garda Complaints will agree to planting evidence."

"But Dermot," she said leaning earnestly across the table, "it's on a need to know basis. Killery doesn't have to know about the real disks, that part of it's none of his business, it's unconnected. And anyway we're not planting evidence, we're just putting it back where it was originally. But he needn't know anything about that. All that can happen after I've been cleared."

109

He still looked dubious, but she realised he was coming round to the idea, either because of his obsession with taking Branden McDowell down or because he genuinely wanted to help her. She didn't care what his motive was . . . well . . . that wasn't quite true. She hoped it was because he wanted to help her.

"I can't do anything today," he said eventually. "I have to go down to Westport to interview Jerome Proudfoot."

"Who's he?"

"I forgot," he said. "You don't know. He's Nicky Power's father. We faxed his photo round the State and Garda Gavin from Westport called me. She said he's been living outside the town for the last five years."

"What about Tony Farrell? I thought he was flavour of the month?"

"Not according to the DNA results or Assumpta Power," he said. "Anyway, that apart, you could always approach Killery yourself and see what he says about your proposition . . . he can contact me when I get back from the West."

"I still say Leonard Power's your man," Grace said. "I'd bet you anything."

Dermot started to laugh. "You're more obsessed with Leonard Power than I am about fucking Branden McDowell," he said and got up to leave.

She put her hand on his arm to stop him. "Thanks, Dermot, thanks for believing me." She said it with sincerity in her voice and he patted the back of her hand and smiled, and saying nothing further headed off to Westport.

Chapter Fourteen

Phoebe was out and the house appeared to be empty when she returned from her meeting with Dermot. She was irritated that Phoebe had taken her request to mind the house so lightly until she went upstairs and found Mungo asleep on the bed in the spare room. He stirred when she entered the room. "Where's Phoebe?" Grace asked. "And I thought you were supposed to be taking Ronan back to school?"

"Change of plan," he said sitting up and running his hands over his bald head. "She took the kid shopping for a computer instead."

"Why?" was all she could say, amazed that Phoebe would even think of shopping at a time like this.

Mungo swung his feet onto the floor and stretched. "The kid's computer was burnt in the fire," he said and went out to the bathroom. Phoebe was beginning to seriously irritate her.

She dialled Killery's number but he wasn't there so she left a message, and then went down to the kitchen and killed time by trying to read the paper. She was agitated and jumpy and couldn't settle, and was about to try Killery's number again when there was a ring on the doorbell. Cautiously she put the chain on the door and opened it. Three large cardboard cartons were sitting on the doorstep together with Ronan.

"Hello again . . . Phoebe sent me on ahead in a taxi with these," he said pointing at the cartons. "Do you mind if I bring them inside . . . I think it's going to rain."

Grace closed the door and took the chain off before opening it again and helping him to carry in the boxes. She stood in the living-room doorway watching him empty out the contents and sort out the spaghetti that was supposed to join everything together. "Where's your mother?" she asked.

The boy frowned. "She said she had a business appointment," he said. "Where can I plug this in?"

She took the flex from him and plugged it into a socket and she wondered if he knew how his mother earned a crust, and if he did, what he thought about it. After further thought she decided that he couldn't possibly know what Phoebe did for a living.

"Here, let me help you," she said taking one of the dangling flexes and attaching it to the correct socket in the back of the monitor. "Do you see much of your mother?"

The boy, who was flipping through the computer manual reading the set-up instructions looked up at her. "Not a lot," he said. Then added quickly, "I mean, she's very busy most of the time you know . . . she has a very important job in the government."

"Yes, of course," she said, suddenly feeling very sorry for this twelve-year-old boy who adored his mother and who was going to be so cruelly disillusioned about her. "Why do you call her Phoebe?"

He looked up at her again and his brow was furrowed. "Because that's her name of course," he said. "What else would I call her?"

Grace shrugged. "Well, Mother perhaps. Why don't you just call her Mother?"

The boy started to laugh. "Because I don't think that'd go down very well . . . do you?"

Grace laughed with him. "No, I don't expect it

would," she said.

Mungo stuck his head round the door. "You stayin' in?" he asked, frightening the life out of Grace who hadn't heard him come downstairs.

"Don't sneak up on me like that!" she shrieked. "And stop creeping round like a fucking phantom, will you?"

Ronan took a fit of laughing and started repeating *fucking phantom, fucking phantom* over and over again.

Mungo gave her a weary look and said, "Chill out, lady, and mind your mouth in front of the kid."

Killery phoned her back just before three. She outlined her proposition to him and waited for his reaction. She was more than a little surprised when he seemed quite open to the suggestion, after she talked him out of his initial anxiety concerning Dermot's involvement. She explained why there was no possible way that Dermot would do anything other than try to bring the McDowells down.

When he tried to probe into the content of the disks and how they came into her possession, she managed to fob him off by saying that they had been sent to her anonymously and contained incriminating accounts, which was near enough to the truth.

Killery agreed to talk to Dermot on his return from Westport, and told her to stay at home. He would pick her up the following day, before going on to the various prearranged points round the city.

That settled, she felt relieved and anxious at the same time. And when Phoebe returned just after six, laden with Chinese take-away cartons, she realised that she also felt very hungry.

Much later, when Ronan was in bed and before Mungo came back from wherever, the two women sat at the kitchen table and talked. Grace asked her about Ronan and Mungo.

"Mungo was a friend of Ronan's father," Phoebe said

simply. "I met Travis when I first went to New York in the mid-seventies. He and Mungo had been in Vietnam together." She sat looking at the wall, remembering.

"What was Ronan's father like?" Grace asked. "What happened to him?"

Phoebe shrugged. "He wasn't much good. He just went off one day."

"So why's Mungo still with you?"

"Because I saved his life once when he'd overdosed, I suppose . . . Both of them were pretty weird in those days, I think it was Vietnam. Anyway, after I met Travis we moved in together, then he and Mungo went walkabout like a fucking road movie. I think they thought they were Jack Kerouac or Dennis Hopper or someone, and I didn't see either of them for a few years. They both showed up out of the blue one night and that was when I fell for Ronan, but Travis buggered off again when I told him I was pregnant. Mungo hung around, I think he liked the idea of a baby, or felt sorry for me or something. He had a serious drug habit at the time. I think it helped him to lay some of his ghosts of the war. One day I found him unconscious so I got him to the emergency room where they pumped him out. Then I paid for his drug rehab programme and he's been with me ever since."

"But how did you know Travis was the father?"

Phoebe gave a snort. "Just because I'm a whore it doesn't mean I'm stupid," she said and Grace blushed.

"I didn't mean it that way."

"Of course you did," Phoebe said, turning serious. "At the time Ronan was conceived, I was working in an administrative capacity. I did the bookings and paid the bills, so I'm in no doubt at all who the father was."

"Are you and Mungo involved?"

Phoebe looked at her and shook her head slowly from side to side. "No, we're not, "Phoebe said. "Mungo isn't into women."

114

"You mean he's gay?"

"No, I mean he isn't into women," she said pointedly. "He's impotent. Half his equipment was blown away in Vietnam."

"How awful . . . " Grace said shocked. "D'you think that's why he got into dope?"

"I'd say the war had more to do with it, but who knows . . . who cares?" Phoebe said. "I'm not his shrink. He's useful, he's just a man and I like to use men, that's all they're good for." Seeing Grace's confused expression she went on, "Oh I know what you're thinking. You think they use me, but you're wrong. Anything I get into is on my terms. I'm the user now."

"Is that why you chose your line of work . . . You think you're redressing the balance?" Grace said, unable to hide the incredulity in her voice.

Phoebe's tone changed from glib to defensive. "Yes, I do . . . Every man I've ever met has tried to use me in one way or another. They're a different species, never mind gender. From my father down," she added acidly.

"I thought you got on well with your family."

Phoebe started to speak, than changed her mind. She sat slumped at the table with her head in her hands for a while, then said, "I don't want to talk about it."

"Come on . . . you've started now."

Phoebe looked up at her. "Why are you so interested anyway. What's it got to do with you?"

Grace shrugged. "I'm just curious. My own old man was a control freak, but it didn't predispose me to be a prostitute."

"Don't be so fucking smug! What do you know about what makes me tick or predisposes me to do anything? You know nothing about my life. Did you have to struggle to bring up a child on your own? Did your own father abuse you and drive you away? People like you make me sick. You're all full of shit and double standards. What's the difference between what I do and the women who sleep with men in return for presents or a car or jewellery? Go on . . . what's the difference?" She was half standing, half sitting, leaning her hands on the table-top glaring at Grace, her voice was heavy with emotion, the air heavy with tension.

"Your father abused you! How? I mean sexually, or what?"

"There's more than one type of abuse. That's another thing that pisses me off. It's assumed that psychological abuse isn't too serious . . . kids can get over being yelled at. Well let me tell you it's just as bad . . . He never forgave me for not being a boy, nothing I ever did was good enough for him. Well maybe I'll just let you bust me, it would be nearly worth it to see his face when the story's splashed across the Sunday papers."

"I can empathise with that, to a certain degree," Grace cut in. "The part about nothing being good enough anyway. My old man was the same with me. And my mother. He makes her life hell. I don't know why she stays with him."

"Well then . . . you of all people should know how I feel."

"I know how you feel but . . . "

The phone rang and Grace went out to answer it. It was Dermot. "You should be home free by tomorrow evening," he said. "Killery talked to me and it's all set up."

"What happened in Westport?" she asked.

"Oh yes . . . Proudfoot's lived there this past five years. He has no alibi for the days in question but in any case he's the wrong blood group."

"So he's not Nicky's father. I knew it. I knew it was Power," she said. "Are you going to demand a DNA fingerprint from him?"

"That's pretty academic at the moment," Dermot said. "He's still unconscious, and the hospital won't let us talk

116

to Nicky's mother yet, but I suppose neither of them is going anywhere."

"When are you coming to get the disks?"

"I'll send a dispatch rider for them first thing," he said. "I want to raid the snooker club while Branden's out looking for you."

"Who was that?" Phoebe said somewhat stiltedly when Grace returned to the kitchen. The atmosphere was less frosty so Grace told her, and of the arrangement with Killery. "Thank God we'll all be in the clear after tomorrow," she said. "And I can get out of here."

"So what are you going to do?" Grace asked her.

"What do you mean *do*?"

"Well . . . is it going to be business as usual or what?"

"Why, are you going to bust me or something so I can make the front of the *Sunday World*?"

Grace said, "No . . . but I was just wondering how long it will be before Ronan cops on to how you really earn a crust. You must have money, but surely there's some other way you could put food on the table."

Phoebe sat at the table and started to trace a pattern with her finger in a small pile of salt which had spilt from the salt cellar. Eventually she said, "I have been giving that some thought. I know I'm getting too old for this game, I'm very close to my sell-by date as it is, so there's not a lot of future left for me, but I don't know what else to do. I mean I don't have that much capital to do anything else, and my expenses are horrendous."

"Of course you have capital, what about the fire insurance on your house, and you must have lots of contacts?"

Phoebe shrugged. "I still have to have somewhere to live for God's sake."

"Yes, but it doesn't necessarily have to be in Dublin 4, Phoebe. Even if you bought somewhere smaller for cash, you'd be bound to have a substantial amount left."

"Are you trying to redeem a fallen woman or something?" Phoebe said sarcastically. "You'll be wanting me to give up the drink next. Anyway, there's a huge mortgage on the house, so there would only be about twelve grand left after I've paid off the building society."

"Suit yourself," Grace said. "I was only thinking of the boy."

Phoebe leapt to her feet and slapped the table hard with the flat of her hand, making Grace jump. "Stop being so bloody holier-than-thou, Grace, you're getting right up my nose," she snapped. "What do you know about anything? And don't try to tell me what's best for my son. I've managed to provide for him perfectly well up to now, thank you very much."

"Like I said . . . suit yourself," Grace said stiffly as she got up from the table. "But if you don't want to break your son's heart, I'd think of something else to do other than your important job in the government . . . I'm going to bed now. Switch off the lights after you."

Phoebe glared at her and as the door of the kitchen closed she stuck two fingers in the air, but wondered why Grace had left her feeling uneasy.

Chapter Fifteen

The dispatch rider called at Grace's first thing and collected the package for Dermot. Killery, on the other hand, didn't turn up until well after eleven, by which time Grace had been to the loo twelve times, and put on and taken off her coat as many more.

"Are you right?" Killery asked when she opened the door. He turned and walked down the path to his car.

Grace followed and sat in the passenger seat. "Where are we going first?" she asked.

"You'll see," he said.

"What's the matter? Are you afraid I'll communicate the destination telepathically to Branden McDowell or something?"

"There's no need to be smart," he said. Killery was very light in the sense of humour department.

Soon afterwards they pulled up near the top of Baggot Street and Killery said, "Get out and walk back to Stephen's Green, to the Wolfe Tone statue, I'll follow at a discreet distance. Wait there until I say."

"Yes, sir," she said, biting back the sudden urge she felt to be sarcastic. But it was a beautiful sunny morning and the trees on the edge of the Green were heavy with blossom. She crossed at the lights, sauntered casually through the Green, and stood beside the patriot's memorial. She looked at her watch, it was eleven-twenty-five. At eleven-forty McDowell still hadn't made an appearance and she wondered which member of the unit Killery had mentally crossed off his list.

She saw him walking towards her and he said, "Back in the car," as he passed, speaking out of the corner of his mouth. She had to stifle the urge to laugh, he was like something from a bad B movie.

"Where now?" she asked when they set off again.

To her surprise he answered her. "Merrion Square . . . I'll drop you at the top corner, walk down to the Mont Clare and stand by the steps." The car slid to a halt and she jumped out and made her way round the square to the top of Clare Street and stood waiting. Fifteen minutes later she saw Kate wandering down the other side of the square. Her heart leapt to her throat until Kate turned the corner and crossed over making for the National Gallery.

Grace wasn't sure if it was just coincidence, or if Kate had seen her and changed plans. She searched both sides of the street with her eyes trying to pick out one of the McDowells or their henchmen. Fifteen minutes later, when no one had approached her, Killery pulled up in the car and they drove off. By the fifth and final rendezvous Grace was becoming worried, what if McDowell didn't show up at all, what would Killery make of that? And was Kate involved? If so why had she gone to the National Gallery instead of waiting for Branden McDowell?

Branden McDowell was conspicuous only by his absence and what Killery thought of it became more than obvious on the drive back to his office. "Nice try, de Rossa," he snapped. "But I think it's time we had a long chat."

Grace's heart sank, she felt angry with herself for being so stupid as to believe that whoever was trying to screw up her life would suddenly follow her script and restore the status quo.

At about the same time as Grace was being driven back to Killery's office, Dermot and four uniformed gardaí were entering Branden's snooker club.

Alan McDowell, who was playing snooker, stopped when he saw the uniforms walking through the front door.

"What's this?" he said looking cocky. "Out in force this time are yeh, McEvoy?"

Dermot took the warrant out of his pocket and slapped it into Alan's hand. "We've a warrant to search these premises, McDowell." He turned and headed for the stairs. "Come on lads, we'll start at the top."

"What d'you expect to find . . . more videos?" Alan said, and stood leaning against the snooker table trying to look cool. Dermot wasn't listening and was half way up the stairs by this time, and when Alan realised this he hurried after him. "Don't waste your fuckin' time, McEvoy . . . there's nothin' here t'find . . . d'you think we're all a crowd of eejits or somethin'?"

Dermot stopped dead at the top of the stairs and turned to look down at Alan. "I'm counting on it, McDowell, I'm counting on it," he said and roared with laughter. Alan looked nonplussed by Dermot's reaction, he was expecting the usual response to his wind-up routine.

Once on the top floor, Dermot sent two of the uniformed gardaí into the storeroom and went with the other two into the office. "Check the desk," he said and went over to the metal shelving. He heard Alan in the corridor outside so he said in a loud voice, "Well, look what I found," and produced the five computer disks. "Switch on that computer, O'Callaghan, let's see what Branden keeps on his electronic toy."

Alan pushed his way into the room when he heard mention of the disks. "What fuckin' disks . . . yeh planted them disks, yeh bastards," he said. He lurched towards Dermot, trying to grab them from his hand, all semblance of cool gone. "Branden's out lookin' . . . "

"Looking for what, Alan?" Dermot said, hardly able to contain himself. He held up the disks and grinned manically. "I think it's time to call in the experts."

Grace wasn't having a whole lot of fun back at Killery's office. He had left her sitting alone for an hour before stomping in and throwing the cash card on the desk, along with her bank statements and the printout from the building society.

"Well, de Rossa, you're lucky," he said. "There are no prints on the card and the building society records and video security tapes show you couldn't have used the card when the two biggest withdrawals were made. And there's no trace of any of the funds."

"Luck has nothing to do with it," she snapped. "I didn't take money from anyone, the first time I saw the card was when you found it at my house, where it was planted."

He sat down behind the desk and lit a cigarette.

"So what happens now," Grace asked. "When do I get my warrant card back . . . when do I get an apology?"

Killery snorted. He stood up and leaned towards her. "If I had my way you'd be out on your arse, woman, never mind an apology. I'm obliged to prove the case against you . . . the onus is on me, and I can't do that. But that doesn't mean that I don't believe you did it, that you've been on the take from McDowell."

Grace was outraged. "I'll prove I'm innocent if it's the last thing I do, Killery." She spat the words at him. "And you'll eat your words, you bastard."

He opened the desk drawer and took out her warrant card. He threw it across the desk at her. "Get out, de Rossa, it makes me sick to have to look at you."

Grace picked up the leather folder, which had slithered across the polished surface of the desk onto the floor. She felt both angry and humiliated and was fighting hard to keep back the tears which she could feel stinging her eyes.

As she got to the door of the office, Killery called after her, "I'll be watching you, de Rossa . . . I'll be watching you."

"Watch all you like, you fascist bastard," she said under her breath slamming the door nearly off its hinges, and thinking that things couldn't possibly get any worse.

She got a taxi home. As she opened the kitchen door she realised that things *could* get worse. Kathleen was sitting at the table deep in conversation with Phoebe. It crossed her mind to turn and flee, but too late. Kathleen jumped to her feet and flung her arms round her neck. "Grace! Where have you been? I've been waiting ages for you."

Grace disengaged herself. "Hello Kathleen, what are you doing here?"

"Well now, there's a welcome for your mother-in-law," Kathleen said, sounding hurt. "I was worried about you, dear, when you didn't come to lunch last Sunday . . . I know how much you were looking forward to it."

"What are you talking about Kathleen?" Grace said. She walked past the older woman and switched on the electric kettle. "I said I wasn't coming. And I don't want to get back with Andrew, whatever you want to think. If you remember, I asked you to mind your own business the last time we spoke and you hung up the phone on me."

Kathleen started to snivel and Phoebe coaxed, "Come on, Grace, there's no need for that. Kathleen was only trying to be nice."

"What would you know?" Grace said glaring at

Phoebe. "She's an interfering old bat. That's the last straw." She slammed out of the room and ran upstairs where she threw herself on the bed and started to sob.

A short time later Phoebe came up. "Things didn't go too well then?" she said sitting on the side of the bed.

Grace heard the chink of a cup and saucer being placed on the bedside table. She rolled over onto her back. "I upset Kathleen," she said, reaching for a tissue. "She'll send me on a another guilt trip now I suppose."

"You could say that," Phoebe said, grinning. "What happened with Killery?"

Grace told her.

"So what's the problem? Your suspension's lifted, they couldn't prove anything."

"That's just the point," Grace said gloomily. "He hasn't said I'm innocent . . . just that he can't prove I'm guilty . . . I can kiss my career goodbye from now on, it wouldn't surprise me if they busted me back into uniform."

"Surely not."

"I bet they do . . . Who's going to trust me to watch their back now?"

"Have you spoken to Dermot yet?" Phoebe asked, almost casually.

"Not yet," she said. "Though I hope his morning went better than mine." She sat up. As she swung her feet onto the floor the doorbell rang and they heard Kathleen trotting across the hall to answer it. Then there was the sound of raised voices and Kathleen screaming. Grace leapt up and she and Phoebe collided in the doorway.

As they reached the top of the stairs they saw Philo Hoban running up to meet them. "Help me . . . help me," she roared hysterically and flung her arms round Grace's knees so that she had to grab the banister to stop herself from overbalancing.

"What is it, Philo? . . . what's the matter?" Grace shouted, shaking the girl by the shoulders to bring her to her senses. Philo started to scream so Grace slapped the girl across the cheek and the scream ceased. "Talk to me, Philo."

Philo let go of Grace's legs and slid down to the top step of the stairs, rubbing her cheek. She looked awful, her eyes were swollen, one of them was blackened and there was a small trickle of dried blood below her nostril. "He's tryin' t' fuckin' kill me . . . You gotta help me . . . you gotta help me."

"OK Philo, calm down. Who's trying to kill you? Is it Branden McDowell . . . did he beat you up?"

"No, I'm talkin' about fuckin' Alan McDowell . . . who d'you think I'm talkin' about? He's after me. I got away from him but he's after me . . . "

Grace shot a look at Phoebe then back at Philo. "OK Philo, calm down. Why was he trying to kill you?"

The girl started to sob so Phoebe sat down next to her on the stair and put a comforting arm round her shoulder. "Did Alan McDowell really try to kill you?"

Philo shrugged and gave a loud sniff. "Sort of . . . He wanted me t' go with a smelly auld fat fella, an' I said no, so he started t' batter me."

"Well I did warn you, but you're safe now," Grace said. "We'll go down to Harcourt Terrace and you can make a statement. We'll pick up McDowell before he can batter you again, though you'll have to press charges."

"An' go t' court?" the girl asked doubtfully.

"Well yes . . . but if you do, he can't touch you again."

"Only if he's put away," Phoebe said between gritted teeth. "You can't ask her to press charges against the McDowells, Grace . . . what if they get bail, which they most probably will. Leave her out of it, you'll have enough with the computer disks anyway."

"He locked me in the club when I said I was leavin',"

Philo whined. "But I got out an' came straight here."

"How did you know where to find me?" Grace said puzzled.

"I heard them talkin' about you . . . Branden went mad and said you had some disks or somethin' an' he was goin' to get them back."

"You mean he's coming here?" Phoebe said alarmed.

Kathleen, who was still standing at the bottom of the stairs, called up to them, "What's going on, Grace . . . Who is this child?"

Grace, irritated with Phoebe for sticking her oar in, ignored her mother-in-law's question. "Shut up, Kathleen. Philo has to bring charges against McDowell, she's a minor and he's forcing her into prostitution . . . he can't be let get away with that."

"That's OK for you to say, you're not the one taking the risk," Phoebe hissed. "And McDowell's on his way over here now."

The front door burst open and Kathleen screamed again as Branden McDowell barged through. He shoved her to one side and waved a Luger pistol in the air. He took the stairs two at a time. "Come 'ere you . . . what're you doin' here," he yelled at the cringing Philo, who was trying to crawl backwards to the landing to escape. He grabbed at her ankle but Grace kicked out at him, just missing his face.

"Bitch!" he yelled. "Where are they?" He grabbed Grace's wrist. "Give me back my property."

Grace twisted free. "Get out of here, McDowell," she yelled back. "I don't have anything belonging to you."

"I saw you, you pair of bitches," he hissed. He levelled the barrel of the gun straight at Phoebe. "And don't think I've forgotten how you shafted me, you whore."

"What's happening?" shrieked Kathleen from the bottom of the stairs. "Who *is* this person?"

"Don't worry about it, Kathleen, Mr McDowell's just

leaving," Grace said, trying to sound under control when really she wanted to panic.

"In my eye, I am," he said. "Not until I get what belongs to me."

"Then you'd better settle in for a long wait, McDowell. By now your computer disks are in Harcourt Terrace being closely examined by your friend Dermot McEvoy."

McDowell looked horrified. "I don't believe you," he said, then turned and ran down the stairs pushing Kathleen out of the way. She went hurtling across the polished floor and ended up in a heap by the front door.

Grace and Phoebe thumped down the stairs and picked her up. "Are you OK?" Grace asked her as she helped her to her feet.

Kathleen rubbed her bottom and nodded tearfully. "Who's that awful person?" she asked. "What does he want?"

"Something he thinks that I have."

McDowell picked up the phone and stood with the gun pointing at all four of them. "Stay where you are and don't move!" He dialled and waited. "It's me," they heard him say. "What's this about McEvoy gettin' hold of my computer disks?" He was silent as the voice at the other end of the line spoke to him. "Then you'd better make sure them disks disappear," was his answer. There was a further pause. Then McDowell said, "Fine, but if I go down I'll make sure you come with me." He slammed the phone down. "Get in there," he snapped, gesturing towards the kitchen with the barrel of the gun.

The three women and the sobbing girl sidled past him into the kitchen. "Where's Mungo?" Grace whispered to Phoebe.

"He's upstairs asleep," she said under her breath.

"In all this row?" Grace said stunned.

Phoebe shrugged. "Maybe he took something."

"Quiet!" McDowell barked. "Sit down there, I need time to think." He stood with his back to the half-open door still training the gun on them, beads of sweat were glistening on his upper lip and his eyes darted everywhere.

"Perhaps . . . " started Grace.

Branden snapped, "I said shut it." And Philo, who was sitting at the kitchen table still snivelling, visibly jumped in her seat. "I need time to think."

Silence descended on the room. Branden was looking distinctly twitchy and Grace was uneasy about the way he was waving the gun around, she had no fondness for firearms. Philo snivelled again loudly and Kathleen, whose face had gone a pale shade of green was almost hyperventilating.

Suddenly, without warning, a huge black hand came around the door and grabbed McDowell round the throat. Another grabbed his wrist and twisted his arm up behind his back with a sickening crack. The gun fell to the floor with a clatter. Mungo's bulky shape materialised in the doorway. McDowell let out a high-pitched scream. Grace dived to pick up the Luger.

"What d'you think about the fuckin' phantom now, lady?" Mungo said grinning. He looked straight at Grace.

"Ohmygod," Kathleen said clutching at her chest and crumpling further into a chair. "Who is *this*?"

"It's OK, Kathleen," Grace said grinning back at Mungo. "This is one of the good guys."

"I'll phone the guards," Phoebe said making for the hall. Grace said, "No wait," and pushed past the whimpering Branden McDowell, who was nursing his broken wrist. She made for the phone and pressed the re-dial button.

"Hatchett," said the answering voice and she slammed down the receiver.

Chapter Sixteen

The flashing blue lights of the ambulance and the garda cars brought out all of the neighbours who stood around waiting for some excitement, though they wandered off disappointed when there were no fatalities.

Hugh O'Boyle and Jack Mulloy went to the hospital with Branden McDowell and a garda car escorted the ambulance, siren whooping.

Kathleen was close to hysteria and was being ministered to by Mungo. Phoebe sat painting her fingernails as if nothing had happened and, in the confusion, Philo had disappeared. When Dermot had finished with Branden McDowell, Grace beckoned him into the hall and closed the kitchen door. He was so high he was walking three inches off the floor.

"What happened with Killery?" he asked. "Are you off the hook?"

"In a manner of speaking, though not through Killery's help . . . Branden phoned his bent copper while he was here and told him to lose the disks."

"D'you know who it was?" he asked.

"I pressed the re-dial button after Mungo decked him . . . Hatchett answered."

"Are you serious?"

Grace looked at him gravely. "Deadly serious."

Suddenly he said, "*Shit!* That would explain why no

one turned up this morning. I didn't include Hatchett in the plan, he didn't know anything about it."

"What'll we do? How do we prove it?"

"We could pump Branden to see if he points the finger," he suggested.

"Branden said on the phone that if he went down, he'd bring Hatchett with him."

"Well there you are then," said Dermot grinning. "He'll solve the problem for us."

Grace looked pensive. "That's all very well but it's a bit chancy . . . perhaps you could tell Killery that *you* pressed the re-dial button after McDowell's call and heard Hatchett answer?"

Dermot hesitated. "I don't know . . . " he said doubtfully. "I mean I didn't, did I?"

"For God's sake, Dermot, Killery won't believe me . . . especially after this morning's fiasco . . . Please."

"Well . . . look . . . I'll think about it," he said.

Grace was getting irritated with him. "Don't think too long, Dermot, we don't want to give him time to cover his tracks," she said.

Suddenly without warning he grabbed her arm. "Come on," he said. "Hatchett's in the office alone with the disks."

They fled out of the house and made it to Harcourt Terrace taking the corners on two wheels. Kate O'Grady was at her desk when they burst into the room. She looked up startled, then smiled when she saw Grace. "Good collar, lads," she said. "Nice to see you back, Grace." And Grace felt a wave of gratitude.

Dermot hurried over to his desk and heaved an audible sigh of relief as he picked up the disks and waved them at Grace.

Hatchett put his head round the door. "Where's McDowell?" he asked and then caught sight of Grace. "You're back, de Rossa, Inspector Killery called me to say he'd finished with you."

And the rest, she thought.

Dermot said, "Branden McDowell's at James's, he broke his wrist before the arrest. Mulloy and O'Boyle are with him. I shouldn't worry though, Howard, he'll be going down for a long time with the help of these."

Hatchett just nodded and said, "Good, good," and left the room.

Dermot grinned at Grace again and said to her in a low voice, "I wonder if he'll do the honourable thing and fall on his sword."

"I shouldn't think so," she said. "Remember the burden of proof. He'll wait until he's well and truly shafted by McDowell first. Unless of course you do the needful . . . "

Dermot was still grinning like a Cheshire cat when Garda Sergeant Micky Potter carried in a printer and dumped it up on top of Dermot's desk, where Branden's computer and monitor were already waiting. They all fiddled with the wires and when it was all assembled, Dermot switched on the power. He typed in the password and while they waited, he chose the disk with the extortion racket files on and popped it into the disk drive.

Hatchett walked back in at that point and stood behind Dermot's chair staring at the monitor. Grace watched his face and saw a ghost of a smile appear and vanish at the same instant that Dermot let out a bellow like a wounded rhino. Startled she looked first at Dermot, and then at the computer screen, where, instead of columns of figures under headings, there appeared gobbledegook, meaningless symbols.

"These disks have been corrupted," said Potter calmly, stating the obvious.

Grace picked up the other disks and one by one with mounting frustration, fed them into the disk drive. They were all the same.

"Have you had anything to do with this, de Rossa?" Hatchett said pointedly.

"Don't try and lay that on her," Dermot burst out. "These disks were perfectly OK before I left the office to pick up McDowell. I was just waiting for a compatible printer to do a printout."

"So who was left in the office then?" Hatchett said, looking round at Kate.

"Don't look at me," she said with a shocked look on her face. "I just got back from lunch . . . the office was empty when I came in, honestly."

Grace shot a look at Hatchett again. The tense expression of a few minutes earlier had relaxed.

Then she remembered. She removed the disk in the drive and returned the screen to display the hard disk directory.

"What are you doing, Grace?" Dermot asked as she brought up the Feel Safe Security File.

"I'm just trying something," she said noncommittally. And then selected the split screen option.

"What are you at, de Rossa." Hatchett said agitated again, just as she accessed the copy of the extortion racket file that Ronan had copied onto the hard disk the night that they had broken into Branden's snooker club.

"What is that?" Hatchett asked but Dermot didn't need telling, he recognised the duplicate of the file he had perused earlier in the day. His face changed once again, as he looked at the screen in disbelief, shaking his head. "Good woman, Grace," he said and slapped the desk, knocking the disks to the floor. "Good woman yourself."

"What is that?" Hatchett said again, sounding near to hysteria.

Dermot took pleasure in telling him. "Branden McDowell wasn't as smart as he thought he was. It looks as if he forgot to erase a seriously incriminating file from

132

the permanent memory."

"Let's get a couple of hard copies of this to be on the safe side," Micky said and Grace typed in the command. She watched the sweat break out on Hatchett's forehead and nudged Dermot. They both gave conspiratorial smiles as the printer tap-tapped out the end of Branden McDowell and perhaps a bent Garda Inspector.

They all went for a celebration drink in Smyths a short time later, minus Hatchett of course. The general mood was exuberant and Grace felt more light-hearted than she had for days.

"Are ye celebrating, lads?" the barman asked.

"We certainly are, Jimmy," said Dermot as he got the drinks in.

Jack Mulloy and Hugh O'Boyle came in from the hospital when the shift changed and joined them, and though Grace sensed a certain coldness from O'Boyle, she decided that she had never really liked him anyway so she could live without his approval. What was causing her more concern was the matter of her record. On paper it was decidedly tarnished and unless she could clear herself completely she could forget any thought of promotion.

Dermot noticed her reflective mood. "Cheer up, Grace, we'll nail Hatchett . . . we got the McDowells against the odds, didn't we? I'll call Killery in the morning."

She smiled at him but had lost the urge for celebration. "I think I'll get back home," she said quietly to him. "I still have to see what Phoebe and Co intend to do, and when I last saw my mother-in-law she was close to hysteria."

"So what's new?" he said as she got up to leave.

Then she remembered Philo. "Did you see where Philo went?"

"Philo? . . . No, I thought you were taking care of that."

Grace shrugged. "Never mind, I'll catch up with her later, she's not in any danger as long as the McDowells are banged up."

When she was out of earshot, Hugh said to Dermot, "I don't expect she felt much like celebrating."

Misunderstanding his meaning, Dermot said, "No . . . I guess not."

Hugh went on, "I mean she'll be fairly well skint now that McDowell won't be dropping her the odd few bob, won't she?"

There was an uncomfortable silence round the table. Dermot knocked back his drink and glaring at Hugh said, "She's back on duty, Hugh, she wasn't the one on the take."

"Is that so . . . Well, there's no smoke without fire I say . . . Who's for another?" He looked round the table.

Dermot stood his ground. "You'll regret saying that, O'Boyle," he said. "I happen to know who is on the take and it's not Grace de Rossa."

"So who is it then, smart arse?" asked Hugh, winking at the rest of the company.

"You'll find out soon enough," Dermot said. He grabbed his coat and turned to leave. "I don't know about you lot," he said to the group, "but I'm fussy who I share a drink with."

After he had gone Hugh said, "What's wrong with yer man?"

Kate got up to leave and Jack Mulloy followed suit.

"I think you pissed him off just a tad, Hugh," she said sarcastically. "I'll tell you one thing though, I'd rather have either Grace or Dermot watching my back than you any day."

After they too had gone, Hugh sat down at the table with Micky Potter. "Jaysus, yeh can't open yer mouth in this place," he said and drained his pint.

Chapter Seventeen

Kathleen was stretched out asleep on the sitting-room sofa with a damp towel on her brow, snoring gently, when Grace arrived home. Phoebe and Mungo were in the kitchen where Mungo was preparing a humungous fry.

"And he cooks as well," Grace said as she sat down at the table.

"As well as what?" said Phoebe.

"As well as breaking limbs."

"He cooks more often than he breaks limbs," Phoebe said dryly.

Mungo said, "One egg or two, ladies?" Grace opted for one, and Mungo served it up along with rashers and sausages and grilled tomatoes.

By the time she had eaten she felt much brighter again. "How's Kathleen?" she asked.

"She'll be OK," Mungo said. "She was just a mite hysterical so I knocked her out." When he saw her appalled expression he added quickly, "I gave her a couple of sleepers, that's all . . . don't blow a gasket."

Phoebe roared with laughter. "I think she was hoping it was a blunt instrument," she said.

"Don't tempt me."

Later as they were washing the dishes the phone rang. It was Dermot. "The hospital says we can talk to Nicky's mother now," he said. "I'll meet you down there."

Ann Power looked even more frail propped up in the hospital bed, and the fact that she had tubes up her nose and a couple of drips attached to her arms didn't help.

"I understand that you saved my life," she said to Grace.

Grace smiled. "I just happened to be in the right place at the right time."

Ann Power's big sad empty eyes stared at her. "I wasn't thanking you," she said without expression. "I didn't want to live . . . you ruined everything."

"Why did you want to die, Ann?" she asked gently, but Ann Power just continued to stare, eyes unfocused.

Suddenly she looked at Dermot. "Where is my father?"

Dermot, who was standing in the shadows by the door, stepped forward. "He's in the next room, he had a bit of a stroke."

"A stroke . . . you mean he's sick?" Grace nodded. "Is he going to die?"

"It's too early to say how badly he's been affected," Dermot said, "but the medical staff say there's a good chance he'll survive."

"Ann. Who was Nicky's father?" Grace asked almost casually.

"Why do you want to know?"

Grace chose her words carefully. She took hold of Ann Power's hand and said, "The forensic evidence confirms that Nicky was killed by her own father . . . we need to know who that is."

Ann looked confused. "How can they know that? . . . it's not possible."

"They know that, Ann, believe me."

"That can't be." She sat shaking her head from side to side, picking at one of the drips in her arm.

"How did your father know that Nicky was missing,

Ann. Did you contact him that morning? Is that why he came to your house so early?"

"No. I couldn't call him, I have no phone. Why do you ask?"

"Because when I met him at your house and you told him that Nicky was missing, he said he'd just heard. How did he hear, Ann? How did he know?"

She frowned and shook her head. "I don't know."

"There was only one way he could have known, if you didn't tell him . . . think about it." Ann Power just stared up at her.

"Ann . . . Who is Nicky's father?" Grace asked again.

Tears were rolling down the woman's cheeks but she stayed silent. "It's your own father, isn't it? Leonard Power is Nicky's father too, isn't he?" Ann Power still didn't answer. She sat staring at nothing, rocking gently back and forth in the same way that Grace remembered her rocking the first morning that they had met.

The night sister put her head round the door, and when she saw the state of Ann Power she walked over to the bed and started to fix her pillows. "I think that's enough for now . . . you can come back tomorrow," she said in the nannyish way that only hospital sisters can adopt without sounding foolish. Then to her patient she said, "Come on, Ann, it's time we had a little rest." Knowing better than to argue the two gardaí left quietly.

"What d'you think?" Dermot said when they were at the top of the stairs.

"I think I'm right."

"So what's new?" he said shrugging his shoulders and turning the palms of his hands up to the ceiling before turning and walking down the stairs ahead of her.

"Well I am," she called after him. She hurried to catch up and they hiked to the car park.

"I'll call Killery first thing," he said. "Though I think it would be a good idea to evict your lodgers. Consorting with a known prostitute and a hit man might not be too healthy for your career either."

She was about to snap back a smart answer until she realised he was only winding her up.

"Thanks, Dermot, you know Killery wouldn't believe me, it'd be more credible coming from you . . . and she's not a prostitute, she's an Executive Recreation Specialist."

He gave her a weary look. As he drove off she searched for her car keys and realised that she had left her bag in Ann Power's room. She cursed to herself and set off back towards the main building. The corridors were quiet and her footsteps echoed so she tried to step lightly.

When Grace reached the room the bed was empty and, assuming that Ann Power must be in the bathroom, she picked up her bag and left the room. Leonard Power's door was ajar as she crept past so she peeped in.

Her heart leaped to her throat. Ann Power was standing by her father's bed holding a pillow over his face. Grace didn't move. The bleep bleep of the heart monitor became irregular. Grace stood paralysed, horrified. Just how Ann summoned up enough strength in her emaciated body to exert the pressure necessary eluded Grace. Later she reflected that it was probably the deep anger that must have been buried in her psyche, surfacing with the grief she was suffering at the loss of her daughter, and directed against the cause of her accumulated misery. The intermittent bleep changed to a long high pitched sound and the herringbone pattern on the screen changed to a single flat line. Grace quietly turned and hurried away. She sat in her car for a long time, stunned into a state of numbness. She felt as shocked as a nun who had accidentally happened upon a naked couple making love.

She couldn't sort out in her mind why she had made

138

no effort to stop Ann Power from ending her father's life and it troubled her greatly. She knew that she had no right to play judge and jury.

She arrived home at eleven feeling jumpy and confused. Her conscience was troubling her, though she had no intention of telling anyone about the act she had just witnessed. Half of her felt that Ann Power's deed was poetic justice, the other half knew that it was a crime and that as an officer of the court she should feel obliged to report it. In her heart she knew that Ann Power had served a long enough sentence already without being dragged through the courts. Leonard Power probably wouldn't have survived anyway, despite what Dermot had said earlier.

Kathleen was still stretched out on the sofa snoring her head off and dribbling from the corner of her mouth. It was not a pretty sight. She could hear a hum of conversation coming from the kitchen but didn't feel like talking to anyone. She was about to slip quietly upstairs when the kitchen door opened and Mungo walked into the hall.

"Hi," he said. "We didn't hear you come in."

Grace gestured towards the sitting-room. "Is she OK?"

Mungo turned and looked in at Kathleen. "Sure . . . she'll be just fine," he said. "You want a drink or somethin' to eat?" She was about to refuse when Phoebe joined them.

"Well . . . are the McDowells well and truly banged up then?" she asked.

"Yes. Well and truly, though they would have walked if it wasn't for your Ronan." She recounted the afternoon's happenings at Harcourt Terrace omitting the part about Hatchett. Phoebe beamed with pride.

"That's my son," she said.

Grace took the bull by the horns. "Speaking of which, I was wondering if you'd made any plans . . . I mean, did you think over what I was saying the other evening?"

"You mean when are we getting out from under your feet? Or when am I going to sign on at the dole office?" Phoebe said with a dead-pan expression.

Grace shrugged. When it came to the point she felt rather embarrassed about asking them to leave when without their help none of the events of the past few days would have been resolved. "I'm not throwing you out on the street . . . really. I was just wondering what your plans were," she finished lamely. She couldn't ask them to leave.

"Go on up and have your bath," Phoebe said. "I'll bring you up a hot drink and we'll have a little chat." That sounded ominous to Grace but she hadn't the energy to argue.

True to her word, Phoebe came up twenty minutes later with a cup of hot chocolate and sat on the side of the bed where Grace was curled up on top of the duvet in her dressing-gown.

Phoebe didn't beat about the bush. "What's the story with this corruption thing?" she asked.

Taken aback by her directness, Grace answered, "I'm hoping it'll be sorted out by tomorrow. I pressed the re-dial button on the phone after Branden McDowell was taken away, so I know who's taking the shilling."

"So what are your plans now?"

Grace looked at her and frowned. "Plans?"

"Well, are you going to stay where you are, or have you ever thought of going into some other line of business?"

"What are you getting at?" Grace asked. "Why shouldn't I stay where I am . . . why would I want to do something else?"

Phoebe shrugged. "I don't know. I just think there wouldn't be much future for you where you are. I mean it seems pretty much a chauvinist stronghold. When did you last see a woman as Garda Commissioner?"

Grace started to laugh. "I'll have you know the Garda Síochána pride themselves on being an equal opportunities employer."

"Oh yes?" smirked Phoebe. "I don't believe in equality myself. Men will never be equal to women, much as they would like to be."

"That's a tad harsh," Grace said. "Anyway I like what I do. I love my job, I wouldn't want to do anything else."

"OK," Phoebe said, getting up. "But if you change your mind I have a business proposition for you."

Grace burst out laughing. "I don't think I'd be any good at your line of work."

Phoebe stopped in the doorway, she wasn't laughing. "I was thinking over what you said about Ronan, and Mungo and I came up with a solution to the problem. An entirely different sort of business, entirely legal . . . anyway if you change your mind let me know, we could do with your expertise." She closed the door quietly after herself and Grace was left wondering what on earth she was talking about.

"Why d'you want to work with her if you think she's so dumb?" Mungo asked when Phoebe sat down at the kitchen table.

Phoebe shrugged. "We may need her, anyway I don't think she's that dumb. And I could learn to like her if it'll get the business off the ground."

"I don't think she's that crazy about you either," Mungo observed wryly.

Chapter Eighteen

Grace got into the office at ten to six the following morning. The place was buzzing when she arrived and the late shift were all still standing around talking.

"What's all the excitement?" she asked Kate who had walked in just ahead of her.

"Leonard Power's dead," she said and Grace tried to look surprised.

"Dead?" she said, her voice rising about three octaves.

Kate nodded. "Yes and that's not all, apparently. Ann Power was found by the night sister sitting on the floor by his bed half out of her mind. She claims to have smothered him with a pillow."

Grace hadn't expected Ann Power to confess. "No kidding?" she said lamely. "When was this?"

"Late last night. You spoke to her. How did she seem to you?"

Grace shrugged. "She was very disturbed. We asked her who Nicky's father was. She wouldn't say, but I suppose this proves we were right all along about Leonard Power. It must have tipped her over the edge, poor soul." She could feel herself beginning to blush.

But Kate didn't seem to notice and went on to say, "If she hadn't confessed the cause of death would have been put down as natural causes. It was touch and go anyway."

"Did they take tissue for DNA typing?"

"Yes. Do you think she'll be charged?"

"I doubt it, taking her mental state into account I shouldn't think that the DPP would bring a case, I hope not anyway," Grace said, though not for the reasons that her colleague may have assumed.

"Did you hear about Hatchett?" Kate asked suddenly.

"No . . . What?"

"He's dead, ploughed his car into a wall at fifty miles an hour. Between you and me, a friend of mine in traffic said he was well oiled at the time."

"What . . . ?" was all Grace managed to squeak, this was not the news that she had been expecting. She caught sight of Dermot at the door of the office, and his expression told her that he too had just heard of Hatchett's untimely and inconvenient demise. She left Kate standing and hurried over to meet him. "Did you phone Killery?" she asked anxiously.

He shook his head. "No, not yet."

"Ohhhhh Dermot," she groaned. "Do it now, please, he mightn't have heard about Hatchett yet."

"It's too late, Grace. It'll just look like I'm slinging mud at someone who can't defend himself."

"Bullshit! The fact remains that Hatchett was receiving corrupt payments from Branden McDowell and was trying to incriminate me," she hissed and waited for some reaction from Dermot, but he stood with his hands in his pockets staring at the floor, saying nothing.

"Dermot, if we don't convince Killery then I'm finished . . . "

"No you're not," he said. "Killery gave you back your warrant card, didn't he?"

"Oh sure! But I can feel the metaphorical glass ceiling crashing round my ears as we speak." Dermot didn't answer.

"So you're not going to phone him ?"

"Look Grace . . . " he started but she cut him off.

"Well fuck you too, Dermot!" she said and stormed off out of the office.

When she had cooled down she called Killery herself. His reaction was exactly as Dermot had predicted.

"But he answered the phone . . . Branden McDowell called him and threatened to blow everything unless he lost the disks . . . "

"Enough!" Killery said. "Howard Hatchett was a first class officer with twenty years service behind him. Don't you have any sensitivity? What do you expect me to do? Go round to his widow before he's even cold and say give me your bank statements, I think your late husband was bent?"

"Well it would be a start, that's your job after all."

"Don't tell me what my job is, de Rossa. I'm well aware of what my job is. It just shows what lengths you'll go to to get yourself off the hook," Killery said coldly. "As far as I'm concerned I know who the corrupt garda is, the only problem I have is that I can't prove it. But your card's marked from here on in, so just watch yourself." He slammed down the receiver before she could say more.

She sat in the canteen for an hour afterwards. Eventually Dermot came to look for her. He sat down and pushed a fresh cup of coffee in front of her.

"What did he say?" he asked without preamble. Grace didn't answer, so he said, "Don't tell me, roughly paraphrased it amounted to, *get lost you bent bitch.*"

"Words to that effect," she said without looking up.

"Did you know that the good Howard Hatchett was Killery's brother-in-law?" he said and Grace groaned. He continued, "I won't say I told you so. If it's any consolation I'd say he knows well you weren't the guilty party, but he's hardly going to jeopardise his sister's pension is he? You should have left well enough alone."

"That's all right for you to say, it's not your ass on the line."

"Nor yours," he said. "Stop making a drama out of a crisis. If you let it go, it'll die a death."

"And I'll stay a Detective Garda for the rest of my career," she snapped. "Probably shifted sideways to an admin post where I can't get up to any mischief."

"Well if you're going to whine about it you can do it on your own time," he said. "As your acting Inspector, I've work for you to do."

"Acting Inspector? I can see why you didn't want to get involved," she said.

Dermot gave a deep sigh and cast his eyes up to the ceiling. "Give it a rest, Grace," he said. "Maybe you should take a couple of days leave until you've sorted yourself out, you're no good to man nor beast in this humour."

"Maybe I'll do just that," she snapped getting up from the table. She was angry and disappointed. She had expected him to support her, or at least take the situation more seriously. Also she hadn't got over the guilt of not attempting to stop Ann Power from killing her father.

On the steps outside she met Philo Hoban on the way in. "Where have you been?" Grace asked, taking her by the shoulder. "I was worried about you."

"I went home. Me ma said I should talk t' you about what them McDowells're doin'. You were right about them. I want t' help yeh."

"I have to go out, Philo, but I'll take you in to see Kate O'Grady. You can tell her about it." Philo was dubious but Grace had no intention of hanging round Harcourt Terrace so she took her inside to Kate and then went to see the only person she could really talk to.

The drive along the coast road to the small fishing village of Dalkey cleared her head a little but she was still in a foul humour. Luckily Faith was home and they went and sat in the garden overlooking Dublin bay and took

145

in the spring sunshine while Grace poured her heart out.

"You are in a mess, Grace," Faith said stating the obvious. "But I don't think you should feel guilty about the Power man, he sounds like he deserved everything he got and wouldn't have lived anyway. And if you're not happy in the job, pack it in and do something else."

"It's not as simple as that . . . "

"It's exactly as simple as that," Faith said. "Life's too short to be stuck in a dead-end job. You'd get frustrated in no time if you thought you weren't going to get anywhere from now on. Anyway what have you got to lose?"

"You mean apart from a regular pay cheque, job security and a pension?"

"Since when did you start counting a pay cheque and a pension as criteria for doing anything?" Faith asked. "If I were you, I'd take what holidays are due to you and look at your options."

"My options are pretty limited under the circumstances. I've only ever done police work and I can't see myself in a Securicor uniform, or in a little hut on a building site in the wee small hours, can you? . . . Besides, you know how I hate dogs."

Faith cast her eyes up to the clear blue sky. "Stop feeling so bloody sorry for yourself. You've got lots going for you."

"Such as . . . ?"

Faith shrugged. "Well . . . you could be a mature student."

Grace snorted. "Daddy dearest would love that," she said and Faith cast her eyes heavenwards again.

"What if he does? Not doing something just because Daddy would approve is rather cutting off your nose to spite your face, isn't it? When are you going to bury the hatchet with him, Grace, he's an old man. He wasn't that terrible."

"Not to you maybe, but what about Mother? He's

persecuted her for years. How can you forgive him for that? He's as bad as Leonard Power in his own way, a total control freak!"

Faith sighed and said patiently, "OK, so you don't, for whatever reason, want to go to college but you could travel, you've no ties after all . . . "

"You mean now that my husband's buggered off with my best friend?"

Faith was now rapidly losing patience. "Look. Just take time to think it over. Something'll come up, you'll see."

"That's easy for you to say."

They sat in silence for a while. Grace didn't want to admit that she was being unreasonable. Faith was trying to avoid an argument. The fresh spring day eventually mellowed Grace and she lightened up a bit and said, "Sorry, Fay . . . I'm just wallowing in self-pity. When I get my head round this I'll be fine."

As she got up to leave Faith caught her hand and squeezed. "Sure?" she asked.

"Sure," said Grace with more confidence than she felt.

Phoebe was on the phone when she got home an hour later. Grace walked past her into the kitchen where she found Mungo reading a copy of the *Beano*. He raised a huge paw in greeting but didn't speak.

"Has the mother-in-law-from-hell gone home?" Grace asked. "Please don't tell me she's lurking somewhere in the house."

Mungo put down his comic and placed his hand on his heart. "The nice lady's gone home . . . cross my heart."

When Phoebe had finished her call she breezed in. "You'll be glad to hear we won't be under your feet for much longer," she said. She looked hard at Grace and asked, "What's the matter with you? You look a trifle tense."

"Well let's say I don't feel like singing zipity-fucking-do-dah," Grace said through gritted teeth and when

Mungo took a fit of laughing, she slumped down at the table and started to cry.

He stopped in mid-guffaw and looking concerned said to her, "Hey, I wasn't laughin' at you, what you said was just funny. What's up?"

"Not a lot," she said through the tears. "It looks as if I'm finished in the only job I know or want to do. My husband wants to whip my house from under me and someone I thought was there for me let me down really badly, that's all."

"So what are you going to do about it?"

"I wish people would stop asking me that," she snivelled.

"Why? . . . It seems to me it's time you stopped feeling sorry for yourself and sorted out what you want to do with your life."

"And it seems to me we already had this conversation a few nights ago," Grace said. "And what have you done about it?"

"Quite a lot," Phoebe said triumphantly. "For one I've got a business plan." She pushed a sheaf of papers under Grace's nose.

"What's this?"

"Read it and see."

Grace read down the page. After a while she looked up and said, "But what do you and Mungo know about detective work?"

"Mungo was in Covert Services in Vietnam."

Grace snorted. "So . . . what good is that? You may not have noticed, but communist guerillas are a bit thin on the ground in Dublin. Anyway, why are you showing me this?"

Phoebe pulled her chair round beside Grace. "With my contacts, Mungo's muscle and your expertise we could run a very successful detective agency. Where's your sense of adventure?" Grace just stared at both of them, stunned into silence. Phoebe went on, "Look, I'll have about twelve grand left out of the insurance after I pay off the mortgage. I could raise another few thousand selling the site and a contact of mine has offered us a whole building on Baggot Street for a ridiculous rent. What about if you sell your share of this house and come in with us . . . the building has four floors, plenty of room for all of us and a good office . . . "

Grace was still sitting with a dead-pan expression. Phoebe lashed on regardless, "We could have a security consultancy as well. You know, the poacher turned gamekeeper approach," she said looking pointedly at Mungo. She continued to prattle on, but Grace had stopped listening. Ridiculous as the idea sounded, it was beginning to grow on her, but she didn't want Phoebe or Mungo to suspect that just yet. She wanted them to work a lot harder to convince her.

Dermot called later in the day to see how she was. She was a little cool with him at the start but thawed out when she saw that he was genuinely worried about her.

"I'm sorry I didn't get to Killery, Grace, but you know how it is. If I could turn back the clock . . . "

"I know, Dermot, I know it's not your fault and I'm sorry if I over-reacted. Anyway it's all academic now, I'm finished in the job one way or another."

"Not necessarily . . . " Dermot started. But she butted in, "Get real, Dermot . . . I'm never going to make Garda Commissioner, am I?"

"So what'll you do? . . . You've no useful qualifications, I can't see any prospects outside for you."

Grace's hackles rose immediately. It was all right for her to express those sentiments but who the hell did Dermot think he was? "Well actually I've already been headhunted," she snapped. "And I'm seriously thinking of taking up the offer. In fact," she went on, "I was just going to write my letter of resignation when you arrived."

"Headhunted? Who by? To do what?"

Having built up a head of steam, Grace pressed on, "A new up-market investigation agency, actually . . . Smart arse."

Dermot looked impressed. "Then I take it back . . . well done. Who are they, anyone I know?"

When she told him his mouth flapped open with shock. He kept repeating, "You're mad in the head . . . mad in the head, woman . . . You've totally lost it . . . lost it." He tried to talk her out of the idea for a while, but the more he tried to reason with her, the more stubborn she became.

As they stood at the front door as he was leaving she suddenly remembered her bet with Jack Mulloy. "Tell Mulloy I'll drop in for my sixty quid tomorrow."

"What sixty quid?"

"Fifty plus my tenner . . . the bet."

Dermot burst out laughing and she was glad that they were parting on good terms. "I'm sure he'll be delighted when I remind him," he said over his shoulder as he walked down the path.

"What was the matter with him?" Phoebe asked after he had gone. "He looks as if someone just told him he's been voted in as the next Pope."

"I think that would have been less of a shock. I just told him that we're going into business together."

"We are?" Phoebe looked delighted and holding up the palm of her hand said, "Gimme five, partner!"

Grace smiled and slapped her hand high against Phoebe's, then started to laugh out loud as she imagined Andrew's face when she introduced him to her new business partners. She tried to drown the slight feeling of apprehension that was beginning to creep across her chest.

THE END